SIXTY FEET UNDER . . .

There was a creak, then an ominous shifting sound, then a slab of rock dropped from the roof of the tunnel onto the floor about a meter behind us.

The dust settled slowly. The small area remaining was dark except for a reddish glow at the edge of the slab behind us. I directed our Torch beam toward it. A bend of elbow stuck out from under pieces broken from the slab. The glow was from a Torch in the enemy soldier's hand.

He was dead. *We* were trapped, which might mean the same thing . . .

WINTER WORLD
by C. J. Mills

Don't miss EGIL's BOOK, the story of Halarek's body-guard facing the ultimate challenge of Winter World.

Books in the WINTER WORLD Series
by C.J. Mills

WINTER WORLD
EGIL'S BOOK
KIT'S BOOK

BRANDER'S BOOK
(coming in January)

WINTER WORLD

KIT'S BOOK
C.J. MILLS

ACE BOOKS, NEW YORK

This book is an Ace original edition,
and has never been previously published.

KIT'S BOOK

An Ace Book / published by arrangement with
the author

PRINTING HISTORY
Ace edition / August 1991

ISBN: 0-441-89445-3

Ace Books are published by The Berkley Publishing Group,
200 Madison Avenue, New York, New York 10016.
The name ''ACE'' and the ''A'' logo
are trademarks belonging to Charter Communications, Inc.

PRINTED IN THE UNITED STATES OF AMERICA

10 9 8 7 6 5 4 3 2 1

To Andy, John, and Ruth,
who've been patient.
Most of the time.

KIT'S BOOK

CHAPTER 1

An officer in the dark uniform of the household Blues thrust aside the curtains to the Lharr Halarek's bed.

"My lord—"

The golden eyes of the wiry man in the bed flew open. He had a stunner trained on the officer before the man could blink twice. The two men remained frozen in position for a few seconds, then Karne Halarek flicked the stunner off and laid the weapon on the bed beside him.

"Sorry, Jenkins. I wasn't entirely awake."

The officer relaxed visibly. "At least you were awake enough to hold your fire, my lord."

The Lharr grimaced ruefully and sat up. "At least that. What would I do without one of the few officers I trust completely? What's happening?" He shook his head as if to clear cobwebs from it, then ran a thin brown hand through his dark brown hair.

Jenkins rubbed the back of his neck and cleared his throat. "I bring very bad news, milord."

Karne Halarek's hands closed into fists, but that was the only sign of tension in him. Inside, he was vibrating with apprehension. It's Kit, he thought. I know it's Kit. Just when things were finally beginning to go right for this House.

Jenkins cleared his throat again, turned away, then turned back, but he would not meet his lord's eyes. "The wedding procession, my lord. The wedding procession was attacked in that cluster of hills southwest of the Great Swamp. The Lady Kathryn was taken. Arl deVree and everyone else was killed."

So Kit and her bridegroom did not even reach deVree Holding and their wedding night.

"How came we by this news? Did House Harlan or House Odonnel call and gloat?"

Jenkins shook his head. "No, my lord. One of the rear guards escaped when he saw how the attack was going." He saw the frown gathering on Karne's face and raised a warning hand. "No, milord. He's no coward. He's sore wounded. The attackers pursued him to our border and our perimeter guards are the only reason he lived to tell what he saw. They fought off the pursuers. The attackers chased him as far as that, milord."

Karne stared at the gray stone floor, but in his mind he saw the hills and the Great Swamp and the open plains between there and Ontar manor. "They wanted no witnesses."

Jenkins nodded vigorously. "That's why the man didn't stay to fight, milord. He felt sure that if he didn't escape, no one would ever know what happened."

Karne took a deep, unsteady breath and looked up at Jenkins. "Obviously he was right." He added under his breath, "Thank God for a talented horse breeder."

Karne stood, flung on the dressing gown lying at the foot of the bed, walked to the door to the Larga's quarters, and pressed the small rectangle beside it several times. *If that call doesn't wake Orkonan, I'll do it myself.* He looked at Jenkins. "Is the man in any condition to talk to me?"

"Not at the moment, milord. He's in surgery. Dr. Othneil says in eight hours or so he'll be in condition to talk more. Maybe."

Karne sighed. "Thanks, Jenkins. Go get yourself something to eat, but stay in the manor after your shift ends. Tane or I may have more questions later."

The pilot saluted and left. Karne looked into the Larga's

room a moment. Neither the Larga nor any of her ladies-in-waiting moved.

They're all asleep. Just as well. Lizanne will have hysterics the moment she hears.

He shut the Larga's door and glanced at his own stark room, his eyes not really registering anything but the painting of Heimdal at the Rainbow Bridge that Egil, his friend and classmate at the Academy, had painted. The Lharr's room was a cold place, by his sire's design. Trev Halarek had despised everything that even suggested femininity or softness. The manor was a cold place, too, and Karne had been too busy fighting off enemies in the four years since his return to Starker IV to change that. Kit had been the only warmth in the manor since their mother's murder. Now Kit had been taken. Lizanne—

Karne pushed thoughts of his timid, sickly wife from his mind, opened his door to the library, and hurried down the winding iron ladder to the library floor. A quick look around the room told him his House administrator had not yet arrived. He tried to stay calm, but fear hindered him. He began pacing the perimeter of the room to wear off some of the emotional energy. He *had* to wear the energy off. A Gharr lord did not break down in front of his employees. A Gharr lord did not break down. But how could he make himself act calm about what had happened? Not for the first time, he cursed his sire's contempt for him, contempt that had resulted in his sending Karne off-world to school. After all, Trev had had his three other sons. Karne would never need to rule.

"Well, I'm ruling now, sire," Karne muttered, "and because of you, the training I have is the opposite of what I need to survive here. I'm learning, but every bit of knowledge has to come the hard way. Men die because you kept me ignorant!"

He stopped in front of the library's massive stone fireplace. Instead of bleeding off his fear and the agony of not knowing what was really happening to Kit, pacing seemed to be adding anger to the mix. Maybe movement was *not* what he needed just now. Karne waved a hand at the fire laid in the fireplace. Realistic flames leaped up instantly, accompanied by the scent of burning wood. He flung himself into the wing chair beside the hearth and stared at the fire.

Gone. Kit's gone and her bridegroom's murdered. Maybe she's been murdered, too. No, no one kills women. They're too scarce. Richard Harlan killed Mother, true, but he was insane with rage at the time. That was an aberration even for him. He's usually far cleverer. But Richard's an aberration in more ways than that. A head-of-House has never been sentenced to prison for murder before either, even though the ''prison'' is the Retreat House at Breven, and the murder was punished only because he had committed it before the entire World Council!

For a moment, remembered grief choked Karne. The Larga had been his teacher and adviser in the politics and customs of the Gharr, politics and customs he had tried so hard to forget during his exile at the Academy on Balder. Politics and customs he suddenly had to know again when Richard had succeeded in killing Karne's sire and all his brothers. Politics and customs that could kill him and wipe out his House.

Focus! Focus your thoughts, by the Guardians! Kit's what's important right now and there's something going on here besides the clan feud. Neither Harlan nor Odonnel is bragging about kidnapping, or calling to name a ransom. There's something else going on, something important, or the attackers wouldn't have risked alienating a powerful neutral like House deVree by killing its Heir.

Karne stared unseeing at the bookshelves across the room. *God forbid Harlan really intends to have her himself! Guardians! Would Breven's damnable Odonnel abbot actually let Richard bring a woman into a Retreat House? I thought Council was keeping a much closer eye on Richard since his escape.*

Karne pounded his fist into the padded arm of the chair, then sprang up and began pacing round and round the room again. *House Harlan is behind this, somehow. And I've not only lost Kit, I've lost a valuable alliance to House deVree. God, you know I value Kit above everything in the world except this House. More than this House. But as Lharr, I have a blood duty—*

The heavy main door to the library thudded shut. Karne looked up. Tane Orkonan, the Halarek administrator, came in with his cousin Gareth and General Wynter. Gareth had been apprenticed to Orkonan four years now and would take a record of this meeting. All three nodded respectfully in Karne's direction, crossed the room to the long library table, and stood there, squinting against the "daylight" level of light in the room. Karne noticed their discomfort with sympathy. They had not been awake long. The sudden change from the "night" light in the halls to "day" in the library would, of course, be hard to adjust to.

"My lord"—Orkonan motioned to the chair at the head of the table—"we can talk better if we're all in one place."

In spite of himself, Karne smiled a little. Yes, it probably would be difficult to discuss a vital matter when one of the people involved was whipping around the room. His amusement lasted only a second. Some action had to be taken at once, both for Kit's sake and to maintain the image of a strong lord which he had built laboriously over the past four years and which was not yet set in everyone's mind. He sat, and the others followed his example. He summarized quickly what Jenkins had told him, then looked at Wynter.

"I want a force of Blues at the attack site by dawn, Wynter. Maybe we'll find some evidence of who took her or where they went. What else do you think should be done?"

Wynter rubbed the back of his neck and closed his eyes for a moment. "I think you should call in Brinnd. Yes, I know he's retired, but he served this House far longer than either Orkonan or I have. Harlan's behind this somehow, and I don't think you'll be able to prove it."

"Send a messenger for him, Karne," Tane added. "You can't trust even a secured tri-d transmission right now."

Karne nodded. "And what can Brinnd do that the three of us can't?"

The spare, graying military man leaned forward. The intensity of his concern was almost palpable. "He knows the political ins and outs better than either you or I do. He knows which chains you can yank in Halarek's present financial and political position and which you'd be foolish to touch just now." He added under his breath, "I wish Olafsson hadn't gone home."

Karne wished the same thing. Egil was a superb tactician, one of the best the Academy had ever produced. He had gone back home to finish his education so he would have the credentials to use his abilities. Karne's own Academy training had been as a pacification officer. He had been very good at it, but those skills were useless on Starker IV, which considered peacemaking cowardly. Having a lord who was thought cowardly was almost enough to bring a House down. Karne was caught, again, in the trap of his sire's prejudice and contempt. Karne's fighting skills had been greatly sharpened by four years of battles and by Wynter's teaching, but they were no match for the skills of the other lords, who had been practicing them since they were toddlers.

"We don't have Egil and we don't yet have Brinnd. What if we can't track her—" Karne slapped an open palm on the table and stood abruptly. "Enough of that kind of thinking. Kit *must* be found. If Halarek is to have heirs—" He stopped. Right now, Kit was Halarek's only hope of heirs. This was not the sort of thing one talked about except with Family, though Karne knew even the kitchen serfs talked about it among themselves. Lizanne had yet to produce a living child. Two years and three pregnancies with nothing to show for them!

Not now. Don't think about that now! When Kit's back safe . . .

Yet every day that went by without an heir in the direct line put all Halarek in danger. If Karne should be killed before producing an heir and Kit be missing, Council would appoint a new head-of-House and that new head would likely, even with Richard in prison, be selected from among Harlan's allies and friends. House Harlan held the votes among the Nine Families and minor Houses, and the Freemen considered appointing a head-of-House Family business. More fools they.

"Wynter, send someone for Brinnd, then get a force of Blues to the site. An attack that killed forty-three people had to leave a lot of evidence behind.

"Tane, send a message to House Durlin. Netta and Kerel's sons must be protected at once and until Kit is recovered. If this is an attack on the succession, as it now seems to be, those two boys must not be reachable.

"Gareth, transcribe your notes, then notify Council Chairman Gashen. Tell him what appears to have happened to the Lady Kathryn and send him a copy of the soldier's statement."

"He'll say this is a Family matter, milord."

Karne looked sharply at the young man, who turned white. It was not acceptable for junior staff members to comment on their orders, especially to their lords.

"Excuse my impertinence, milord," Gareth mumbled.

"Excused. Remember not to do it again."

The young man bobbed his head and hurried from the room. Karne watched him until the side door banged shut behind him. Gareth would know that in many other Houses such a comment would have cost him his tongue, and he would not make that mistake again. Karne had found, contrary to the general belief on Starker IV, that mercy toward servants in such circumstances resulted in greater loyalty and obedience, not less.

Not that I could order a person's tongue cut out, anyway, Karne told himself, but the servants don't necessarily know that.

Wynter had gone. Orkonan had left for the tri-d room. Now Gareth, too, was gone. It was time to dress for the coming search. He could imagine Wynter and Orkonan's protests that he should not risk himself, that he was the ruling lord, the last Halarek, etc., but how could he sit in the manor, safe and warm, while the-Guardians-knew-what was happening to Kit? A brother's place was at the head of the search. He ran up the iron stair to his room.

CHAPTER 2

Karne brought his flitter in low over the end of the Great Swamp. He dipped the craft's wings once to indicate to the troop transport and the other fliers with him that it was time to land. By prearrangement, all but two of the accompanying fliers were to land to one side of the battlefield. Karne, with Phillipson and Obren, two trusted pilots, planned to track the attackers from the air.

Karne circled the site. The soggy turf had been churned up by many hooves and feet. A few men in Halarek blue and many, many more in deVree's light orange uniforms sprawled, dead, along the road. The banners and ribbons that had made the procession so gay and bright as it left Ontar lay trampled into the mud or tangled around corpses.

So many dead, and all for the sake of tradition, Karne thought bitterly. Another Starker IV custom that should have been ignored: the wedding procession from the bride's holding to the groom's.

Karne had had no say about the procession, because authority over Kit had passed from Karne's hands and from his House to House deVree as soon as the pastor had received the couple's vows. He had argued with the duke. He had tried to convince him that, fine fall weather or not, conditions were too dangerous to follow the ancient custom. He might as well have saved his breath. The duke was courteous, but firm in his belief that custom must be followed. There could be very little risk, he had insisted. Richard was in prison, after all, and Odonnel never acted without Harlan.

DeVree was already blaming Karne for the massacre. The duke had been livid when Karne notified House deVree what had happened. Did Halarek have some secret feud with another House? the duke wanted to know. DeVree had no important enemies. Or was this how Karne changed his mind about the wedding? Karne had swallowed the insults in silence. The duke would be sorry later and would apologize. And he would have the rest of his life to regret his decision in favor of the wedding procession, because the duke also followed another ancient custom of the Gharr: The head-of-House and the Heir never travel together.

Karne's thoughts ran back to the kidnapping. Had Richard Harlan been free, Karne would have laid the blame immediately at his door, but Richard was in solitary confinement at the Retreat House at Breven. Some Harlan cousin or vassal had arranged it, then. Or perhaps House Odonnel. That House might try to increase its prestige while Richard was confined, or try to curry favor with Richard. Only the Guardians—or perhaps Richard Harlan—knew how Garren Odonnel thought. There was an off chance that House Kingsland could, but Ingold Kingsland, ruthless as he was, would not cross Richard. Not after Ingold had arranged for his sire to have an "accident" so he could become head-of-House and ally Kingsland more closely with Harlan.

But right now, *who* had taken Kit did not matter nearly as much as *where* they had taken her. *Who* could be puzzled out later. Pray the Guardians they found her before the storms of Uhl closed the planet down for the winter. Kit in the hands of a Harlan ally for an entire winter did not bear thinking about.

Karne brought his flitter closer to the ground and skimmed northwest along the trail the attackers had left. Phillipson's and Obren's flitters followed him. Out of the corner of his eye he saw that the other Halarek flitters and the troop transport had landed safely near the ruins of the procession.

That transport will have a grim load to take back, he thought.

The trail left by running horses changed from churned, wet mud to clods of earth torn out of drier ground to a wide path of crushed brown grasses leading into the hills. There had been a lot of men. A hundred, at least, maybe more.

Phillipson's voice came on suddenly, loud over the com. "Lord Karne, look, on your right."

Karne craned his neck to see out the passenger-side window. A scorched circle lay just out of sight of the road behind the first of the hills. Farther up the valley beyond it lay another and another and then two very large ones, made by nothing smaller than a troop transport.

"Thanks," he said, and dropped his flitter onto the dried grasses near one of the larger marks.

There was no use in getting out and looking. He knew that before he opened the flitter door and hopped out onto the wing. But he had to do something, to *feel* like he was doing something. This was a dead end. There was no way to trail fliers. Starker IV had no central air-control system like the more civilized worlds of the Old Empire and the Federation did. Oh, no, that would infringe too much on the freedom of the Houses to fly where they wished when they wished, unguarded, unwatched, unreported. The fact that most professional assassins flew to near their targets to save time had nothing to do with the reluctance of the Nine Families to consider a central flight control system. No, of course not.

Karne waited until Phillipson and Obren had landed, to avoid being burned by their backwash, then jumped down onto the frost-crisped grass. He kicked a stray rock viciously. The other two pilots jumped down and began inspecting the smaller landing areas. Every once in a while one of them crouched and picked something up from the ground. Sometimes the pilot kept what he found, sometimes he dropped it back into the grass.

Karne paced the diameter of the scorch. Definitely a troop transport, and a big one. It would have had to have been big to carry all those horses. This had not been a random strike by an unusually large band of outlaws. Karne had never seriously considered this possibility, but some of his officers had. Out-laws, however, would probably have killed everyone, even a woman, and taken what valuables they found. Or they would have left the woman alive but wishing she were not. No, this had been done on horseback for pinpoint accuracy. Kit had been the target and striking from horseback usually avoided serious mistakes that sometimes occurred in air attacks, like killing the Heir of a major House. If killing Arl had been a mistake.

Karne crouched on the far edge of the burned mark and looked across it. He could see only the backs of the hills. Even this large assembly of men and animals would have been hidden from the procession on the road until too late. The duke's men had been lax, though. Unforgivably lax. Outriders should have found these machines long before the main procession got any-where near.

Of course, outriders might have found the fliers and been slaughtered before they could pass the news. They would have been appallingly outnumbered. The absence of any trace of outriders might also mean that the entire procession would have been packed up and disposed of somewhere else if that guard had not escaped. The attackers had certainly had plenty of storage space to take all the bodies away, if that had been the original intention. That way, Kit would have vanished without a trace. *Who* had taken her? Halarek and deVree would find out only when the kidnapper revealed his price—*if* the kid-napper revealed a price—but Karne now knew how she had gone.

He looked across the scorched places. There were eight of them, including the two transport-sized ones. It took money to arrange that large an array of men and equipment. Karne him-self had never taken two transports out at one time. Was it possible deVree had been offered something to betray Halarek? Karne shook his head. No. Though to be suspicious meant to stay alive on Starker IV, *that* was letting suspicion run away with him. DeVree had never had reason to stand with Harlan. Besides, the duke took sides only on principle. There would be no bribing him. Even if someone *had* found a means of coercion, that person surely had not told the duke his son would die. The duke, like Odin Olafsson, Egil's father, loved his children.

Karne stood. He looked questioningly at Phillipson, then Obren. Phillipson shrugged and held out empty hands. Obren shook his red head slowly. Karne trudged back across the burned circle, his boots sending up little puffs of gray, charred-grass-smelling smoke with each step. He would have to wait for word to come from the kidnapper.

When he reached the other men, Obren held a bridle ring toward him, and a fragment of stirrup cover. Neither was anything out of the ordinary. There would be no tracing the attackers from them. Phillipson shook his head, and his voice held as much sympathy as one Gharr man could show to another.

"She's a valuable hostage, Karne. She'll be found. Or at least you'll be told she's alive and well."

Karne nodded and turned toward his flitter. Obren fell into step beside him and let his large, freckled hand rest comfortingly on Karne's shoulder for a moment. "I have a little sister, too, milord," was all he said.

As soon as Karne returned to Ontar, he went to the library, the usual place for Holding business. There had been no word from the kidnapper. Karne had not expected any, but he had hoped. There was word from Brinnd, though. Gareth presented it to Karne with some trepidation.

"Frem Brinnd could not come himself, milord. He sent this letter back with the messenger." The young man thrust a recorder toward Karne.

Karne looked up at the young man. Gareth shifted his weight from one foot to the other. Karne looked away. *He's so eager to do things exactly right that he takes my slightest deviation from customary behavior as a criticism. Dear God, was I ever that young and eager?* He looked again at the young man. *No, when I was seventeen, I was defending this House, trying to convince the Council to put Harlan under trusteeship for laying siege illegally early and without the required notice....*

For a moment Karne thought of Harlan's gang assassination attempt on him over the Desert of Zinn just after he returned from Balder. He and Nik von Schuss, Heir in von Schuss, had been the only survivors of that attack, and that only through

Nik's skill as a pilot. Had that been only four years ago? Karne ran a weary hand through his hair. It felt like ten.

He became aware that Gareth was still standing beside the chair, waiting for orders. "You may go, Gareth. I'll buzz for you if I want anything."

"Very good, milord." Gareth bowed and left the library through the side door.

Karne turned on the recorder and closed his eyes. It was easier to focus on the sound that way. Brinnd's voice, cracking with age now, came clearly into the room.

"My lord Karne, greetings. It's been a long time since we've talked. It will be longer yet, for I'm confined to bed now. Please forgive my inability to come to you. You know my heart has long been with Halarek.

"There is little you can do if you can't find the Lady Kathryn yourself. You realize, of course, the value to an enemy of an heir that is half Halarek, so no one, not even Harlan, will damage her. But the results, for you and Halarek, could be decidedly awkward."

Karne snorted. "Awkward" was probably the mildest word that could apply to the situation. A Harlan/Halarek child, an Odonnel/Halarek child, especially if male—

Kit had a year's supply of preventatives with her—the Lady Agnes had successfully persuaded Arl that Kit's body needed another year to mature before she began producing heirs for deVree—but whether any of her baggage had gone with her was impossible at the moment to say.

Brinnd was continuing: ". . . . young von Schuss. I know why you decided to send him back to his House and it was a wise move at the time, for with him at Ontar the Lady Kathryn would never have allowed the contract with deVree to be made. Halarek needs no marriage to bind it closer to von Schuss. But they love each other. Under ordinary circumstances that would be irrelevant, of course, but love will give Nicholas reason to hunt for her long after men who are ordered or paid to hunt her have lost their enthusiasm. And he as yet has no wife to plague him with jealousy about such a search. Ask von Schuss to come and help. It will be a long hunt, milord. Have courage. You'll need it.

"I and my children and grandchildren pray daily for the

continued good health of Halarek, House and man, my lord. After forty years in the Lharr's service, Halarek is as my own family to me.

"With deepest regards and affection, I wish you all good fortune."

Karne sat still in the chair until the echoes of Brinnd's voice in his mind died away. The old man had been a wise and effective administrator. That he was still willing to share his wisdom was a blessing. Call Nik into the hunt, Brinnd had said. It had been hard to send Nik home, because he had become Karne's best friend since their brush with death in Zinn. But he and Kit had loved each other for almost four years and, clearly, the temptation to touch had been getting too strong for them. In spite of their best intentions and the years of strict training that required them to stay open to marriages beneficial to their Houses, they would soon have yielded.

It would have been too dangerous for them to love and marry, Karne reminded himself, even if marriage between them had been acceptable. If a man loved his wife, he created a weakness: Her kidnapping or the threat of torture for her would make him far more likely to give in to an enemy than he would under more usual circumstances.

Karne thought of his own wife, now abed to prevent a possible miscarriage, the threat caused, so Lizanne said, by her anxiety about him going to the battlefield. She had not been a good match, either, but she was the best he had been able to get at the time, and Halarek had been in desperate need of an heir. It still was. And if Kit were gone for good, as she well might be, Lizanne would be all the personal family Karne had left. Richard Harlan had killed everyone else, except the Larga Alysha, within the legal rules of feud. Karne thought of the ancient nursery rhyme the nursemaids had sung to the Halarek children. One character had had something disastrous happen to it and then another did and then another until there was only one left.

"And then there was none," Karne whispered to the empty room.

CHAPTER 3

They came down on us out of the hills, the Odonnel raiders, shouting and beating drums, of all things. DeVree's outriders hadn't cried a warning (perhaps they were all dead) and my lord deVree, who had thought a large armed guard both unnecessary and inappropriate to a wedding procession, had *flown* home.

Arl fell from his horse as limp as a rag. I knew from the stillness of his body that he was dead. Before I could *feel* his death, someone grabbed me from behind and threw a blanket or sack over my head. I struggled and fought. He slammed his fist into my jaw and everything went black.

I came aware slowly. I heard a rush of air outside the vehicle I was in, felt the subtle shifting of bodies around me, then a bump, and then a sensation of rolling over rough ground. I opened my eyes a slit. It was late morning and the flitter I was in had landed on a ground-level landing pad. Hands unfastened the safety webbing around me, hands that took liberties not permitted to anyone but a lover. I opened my eyes and glared at the florid Odonnel soldier whose hands were holding what they should not touch.

15

"I'll have both your hands for that," I said, as icily as I could manage.

I didn't know what I actually could do about such abuse of authority, but perhaps the soldier didn't know either. Someone with great power had arranged this kidnapping. I couldn't be worse off by attempting to use an echo of that power.

The soldier backed away hurriedly, apologizing fervently, his longish hair almost sweeping the flitter's floor with the abject depths of his bows.

So, my kidnapper was a man who would *actually* take a man's hands. Karne only *says* such things as a reminder to servants of what happens in other Houses, and they do remember. The man's apologies also told me that, though prisoners captured in such attacks are usually treated very roughly, I was not to be. I would not even be insulted by underlings if I stood up for myself.

The pilot himself offered to help me out onto the wing. That courtesy was another sign that I was to be well-treated, and *that* meant my capture was the object of the attack and not mere chance. I looked down at the ground. A troop or more of soldiers, a mixture of Odonnel and Harlan men, stood on the grass around the flitter, surrounding a short man with the fine, high-bridged Harlan nose. House Harlan. Of course. The Odonnel soldiers had just been camouflage. It was so expected a discovery that I didn't even feel afraid at the time. It had been four years since Harlan had directly attacked members of my family. It was time.

I scanned the surroundings. Perhaps I could identify this place. I had to have some knowledge of where I was before I could plan an escape, and I was unlikely to see outside for some time.

The landing pad lay at the foot of a stone tower, probably originally built by the Old Ones, but recently repaired. A stable and a fenced horse-pen occupied the near side of the tower; a gleam of lake water was visible over a low ridge to the other. Tens of kilometers behind the tower, the mountains at the edge of the Frozen Zone began. I guessed it was the north Frozen Zone, since I didn't think I'd been unconscious long enough for it to be the southern one. For one thing, I wasn't hungry enough to have traveled that far.

The Harlan man and his escort came forward.

"Welcome, in Duke Richard's name," the man said, offering his hand to shake in Family fashion.

I ignored the hand and wondered if he used Duke Richard's name to mean I was welcome on behalf of House Harlan or to mean that I would actually meet Duke Richard, who was *supposed* to be firmly confined at Breven. I thought of demanding to be sent home at once, but decided I'd only look silly: House Harlan had been willing to kill several hundred people to bring me here.

"I'm Brander Harlan," he continued, unruffled by my pointed rudeness, "and daymeal is waiting." He motioned toward a massive red door in the foot of the tower.

One of the soldiers hurried ahead to open the door for us. Once inside, fear gripped me. I feared the ancient tower, with its connection with the Old Ones and their tunnels and mantraps. I feared the Harlan man even more. Brander took my elbow and steered me to a dining room with a long narrow table set for three. The homey smell of warm bread and hot klag made my stomach growl and temporarily relieved my fear.

A chunky man of nearly thirty rose from a chair beside the fireplace and came forward. He bent over my hand in the formal salutation of lord to lady.

"I'm Ennis, Lady Kathryn," the man said. "I'm most pleased to see you whole." His voice was bland, but his meaning was not innocent and was aimed at Brander Harlan.

Brander shot him a black look. "Ennis *Harlan*," he said curtly and sat down at the table.

Ennis released my hand and stood looking at me. I returned look for look. He, too, had the Harlan nose. His eyes were golden brown and the upswept wrinkles around them suggested that he had a sense of humor, though his face was deadly serious at the moment. He was only slightly taller than me. His hand had the callouses of a lord who does not let servants do all his work.

He pulled out a chair at the table for me, which was an unusual courtesy, even in Halarek. As he bent to push the chair in, he whispered in my ear, "We've much to discuss, by Lord Richard's command, but not now, and not in Brander's presence."

Richard's name brought the fear back. The food that had made my stomach growl and my mouth water now looked unappetizing. I put a hand on the table to steady myself.

Don't ever show an enemy you're afraid, Mother's voice repeated in my head. *Fear often makes such creatures more likely to attack.*

I swallowed, shut my eyes for a moment, and prayed for courage. Instead, my imagination told me the men could smell my fear. A warm hand, resting just a fraction of a second on mine as it passed the bread, helped. It was nothing Brander would notice. The brevity of contact said it wouldn't be a good thing if Brander *did* notice. I kept my eyes closed a moment longer and let out a small sigh of relief, just loud enough for Ennis to hear, to tell him *I* had noticed and appreciated it.

When the meal was over, Brander settled back in his chair, sipped his drink, and flapped a hand toward Ennis. "Get on with it," he said.

Ennis stood abruptly. "Not here. Not with you."

Brander's eyes narrowed. "Today. Lord Richard commands today."

"I'll take care of it in my own way, in my own time, and *that* means without your insolent presence anywhere near." Ennis's voice was hard and tight.

"The law requires witnesses."

"The law requires *Council* witnesses. *Freemen*. If you have any of those here, I'll use them, much as I dislike the idea."

Brander gave a sharp bark of laughter. "You jest, cousin. Council? Freemen? Here? Under these circumstances?"

I felt Ennis's anger, like a vibration in the air, though he kept it tightly reined. "You arranged these 'circumstances.' I had no part in it. If Richard knew—"

Brander laughed again, an uglier laugh. "You hold Cousin Richard in too great esteem, Cousin Ennis. This was *his* plan, beginning to end."

Ennis went white, then red. "Guardians!" He spat out the word.

He grabbed my hand, pulled me to my feet, and started from the room. Brander set his drink on the table and rose to follow.

"No," Ennis snarled.

"A witness," Brander answered.

"A voyeur, you mean. No Council member means no legal witness. YOU WILL STAY AWAY."

"Richard—"

Ennis seemed to grow larger with the power of his anger. "I'm senior here, and you'll do as I say or I'll have you taken back to the manor!"

Brander sank back down into his chair and lifted his drink in a graceful salute. "Work hard. Have fun," he said and turned his attention to the drink.

Ennis pulled me out into the hall and shut the door unnecessarily hard. He stood there, inhaling deeply and exhaling slowly, ignoring the curious glances of the two soldiers who guarded the door. When the breaths no longer shuddered as they came in and out, Ennis took my elbow and directed me up a flight of stairs and into a comfortable, if masculine, bedroom. He glanced at the bed, then dragged the room's upholstered chair nearer to the fireplace and motioned me into it. I hesitated.

"You'll be better off sitting when you hear what I have to say," he said. "It's going to take a while and you're not going to like any of it."

"Then why bother?" Hours of fear and anger came out in a bitter sharpness.

He gave me a hard look. "Because I'm trying to make what could be a terrible experience for you just a little bit easier. You've had enough pain already. Or are you one of those women who think the purpose of life is martyrdom and suffering?" His voice, too, was sharp now.

I took a deep breath and held it. Sometimes that helps me face awful things. Everyone I knew in deVree was dead, except the duke. Even Arl was dead. I was a widow before I'd really been a wife. Right now, the shouting, the burns, the blood, the memory of Arl falling dead from his horse, were like a bad dream, something that would vanish in the morning. But I knew it had been no dream. In the morning all would be real and I'd *feel* the horror and the pain. In the morning, I'd be in no mood or condition to listen to this man who was trying to help me, enemies though we were.

I released the breath and looked again at Ennis. He was laying sticks and logs for a real fire. The building was truly old if it had a real fireplace. I began to suspect I knew at least part of what he had to say. There was only one Family ritual that required witnesses from Council, Freeman witnesses. Fear made my throat so tight it was difficult to speak. My voice came out a whisper. "No, I don't like pain. I don't like suffering. I was going to have a happy life—" Then, to my dismay, I burst into tears.

Ennis cursed, then he was kneeling beside the chair, his hands holding mine, his voice making comforting noises. His solid shoulder was so close, so available to cry on. I held myself aloof. He was Harlan and, in spite of his kind actions, House Harlan had something very unpleasant planned for me, something Ennis Harlan was going to do to me. But he was offering comfort, and the day's horrors weren't yet over, and I was very afraid. His sympathy undid me, and in the rush of tears and words I ignored his clan and spoke of things usually said to no one but Karne. The words flowed on a river of tears.

"We could have been happy together, Arl and I. We *liked* each other. And he didn't mind my tomboy ways. Not much, anyway. And now he's dead! Because of me!"

"Hush, hush," Ennis murmured. One hand brushed damp hair back from the corner of my mouth. His gold-brown eyes held only concern. "It was in no way your fault. Richard planned it. You heard Brander say that. Hush. Crying can't help. You know the ways of feud."

Outrage dried up the well of tears. "The ways of feud! The feud was none of deVree's affair. *Everyone* that died was innocent! It's Halarek and Harlan's feud. Arl and his Family were *innocent!*"

His face hardened. "DeVree stepped into our feud when he contracted a marriage in Halarek. There was nothing you could have done to stop it without refusing the alliance. What happened is past and done. Now is now and we have to handle it now or Brander and his troop will. I'm senior here, but I rule only as long as everything goes according to Richard's plan."

Ennis stood and went back to the fireplace. He crouched there, arranging sticks and logs in silence, for some time. Even after he had coaxed a fire to life, he crouched there, his wrists hanging limply over his knees. Finally he sighed heavily, stood, and faced me.

"This is the hardest thing I've ever done," he said. He half turned toward the fire and then turned back, as if resolving to face me with this hard thing. He took a deep breath, then the words rushed out. "Lord Richard wants a baby to end the Harlan/Halarek feud. Harlan, my father's House, breeds many more healthy girls than any of the other Houses. My mother's line, too, has high genetic resistance to the Sickness. Halarek has energy and the kind of stubborn courage that's dying out in Harlan. We're like fine, blooded horses, you and I, Lady Kathryn. You're to be my mate, my bride. Today. By Sheet and Broken Seal. Willing or unwilling. God help me, I hope to make you willing, but it's my duty to my House to wed as ordered, just as you did with deVree."

I shut my eyes. For the first time I saw the "ceremony" of Sheet and Broken Seal for what it was: legal rape. That was why Council demanded witnesses, for the protection of the woman's name and reputation. But Sheet and Broken Seal hadn't been used for generations. Not on women of the Gharr. It was only for Black Ship brides. Not me. Not rape!

"No, No, NO, NO!"

The loudness of those words surprised me. That I'd said them aloud surprised me, but the sound made real what was to happen, and soon. I flew at Ennis then, out of control with anger as I had never allowed myself to be before. I attacked him with fists and nails and feet. "How can any man be a part of such a ceremony?" I shouted at him. "How can any man make a fellow human into a *thing* like that?"

Ennis grunted as my weight hit him and flinched as my fist took him hard beside the eye. He grabbed for my hands, caught them, and slowly forced them down and behind my back. Then he pulled me so hard against him that my feet had little swinging room. I twisted and wriggled, rage at my helplessness, rage at being used burning me up. I couldn't break free.

Slowly I realized he wasn't hurting me. Whatever pain I felt would stop when I stopped. Ennis was only preventing me from hurting him. Was it possible he meant it when he said he didn't want to hurt me? That he'd been ordered into marriage with me as I'd been with Arl? I hadn't thought about *men* being ordered into marriage, but it had happened to Jerem and, in a way, to Karne. Karne's duty to Halarek had forced Lizanne on him.

I stopped fighting, looked up, and caught a crooked smile on Ennis's face.

"You and your brothers must have fought a lot, milady. You're very skilled at it and hard to hold." He studied my face a moment, then added, "And it's good you stopped wiggling when you did, or we'd have become man and wife sooner than you'd like and far more abruptly than I'd planned."

Instantly I was aware of a long hardness against my hip. Ennis loosened his grip a little and my fingers tingled as blood ran back into them.

"That's better," Ennis said softly. "I won't hurt you if I can avoid it, Lady Kathryn, and that includes during the ceremony Lord Richard has required of me, but I won't let you hurt me and I will do the duty I owe my Family. Let that much be very clear to you."

There was no way out. Kindness only went so far. It was a shock to recognize that, deep inside, I'd expected to escape that ritual. I'd expected it until I heard and felt Ennis's determination to obey his head-of-House. I'd expected it, even though I'd obeyed *my* head-of-House the same way when I signed the deVree marriage contract. Arl would never have hurt me. This man had also promised not to hurt me *if* I let him take me. Tears began again and I couldn't make them stop.

"I was married only this morning, this *morning*, and now Arl is dead and you want to force me into another marriage without leaving me any time for grief."

Ennis touched a tear as if in wonder. "You grieve for him? Though he was your brother's choice?"

I nodded. It was all I could do. Words would have choked me. Arl was so newly dead that it was hard to believe he was dead. "Arl was kind to me and tolerant," I finally managed to say. "He wouldn't have beaten me when I disagreed with him or disobeyed him. Most of my other suitors would have. So I—I—felt affection for him. We would have had a good marriage."

There was no speaking of the kind of marriage I could have had with Nik. That match had always been out of the question.

"Then I'm even more sorry that I had any part in this."

Ennis stood with head bent, thinking, then he let go of my hands and gripped me firmly by the shoulders, more for emphasis, I think, than for control. "I'm twenty-seven years old and have no wife because there are no women available to me here and I can't afford a Black Ship. I thought I'd die without children, until Richard offered me a rich and well-connected bride. I wanted a wife. I wanted children. I swear before God I didn't know what he intended to do to get them for me. I swear before God! Though I could've guessed, if I'd wished to. And to attack a wedding procession!"

A sick look crossed his face. He dropped his hold, spun away, and stood with bent head and drooping shoulders. He looked conscience-stricken. He said he hadn't known, and I believed him. He was Harlan, yet I believed him. If this was a performance, it was very convincing.

At last he turned around, but he didn't move closer. "We will be man and wife by morning." His voice was still determined, but it held a little sadness now. "It's my duty to obey the head of my House and I will do that this afternoon, as you did your head-of-House this morning. There's no way you can prevent me. You can only make the process painful for yourself. I know to yield willingly to me will be almost impossible for you, but it's what I'm asking. I know I'm an absolute stranger and from an enemy House besides, but please, please, let me make what has to happen at least comfortable for you."

I didn't know what to say. If I lay with him without resisting, then I betrayed Halarek. If I fought him, he would take me still and I had still betrayed Halarek. If there was any other alternative, it was death. "Please," I whispered. "I can't think. So much has happened . . ."

"I know."

Did I really hear sympathy in his voice? "Can I have a little time?"

His mouth twisted upward in a wry smile. "Several hours, perhaps, but not more. My impatient cousin will probably want proof the deed is done long before morning." His look sharpened. "You *are* a virgin?"

I couldn't help stiffening, though it was a normal question. DeVree had even required that a physician certify I was still intact. Still, this was not a normal situation and the question *felt* offensive. "Of course," I snapped. "How else could my husband know—have known—the first child was truly his?"

"That's the spirit!" Ennis smiled, though I could see he was still tense behind that momentary warming. "I thought that would stop the tears. Come, I'll show you a good place to think." He motioned toward the door. "McNeece picked a great place to set a hunting lodge."

I stopped in mid-step. "McNeece? Van McNeece?"

He must have read on my face the dismay I felt. "No, he doesn't know anyone connected to Harlan has rented this. But his estate manager does. Think, my lady. Were you the Lharr Halarek, would you consider a McNeece property a likely place for Harlan to hide the Lady Kathryn?"

The diabolical cleverness of the hiding place hit me. I could be held here until the spring hunting season and no one would even think to look here. Everyone knew how strongly anti-Harlan Van McNeece was. Ennis had also, by naming Mc-Neece, told me where I was. Home was south and east, across the plains. Had Ennis meant to tell me, or had he just been careless? Or was the lodge so well-guarded that he need not worry I'd get out? I could puzzle that out later. I had a more pressing matter to think about.

Ennis took me to the top level of the tower, to a room with windows on all sides. It had no furnishings other than a few scattered rugs of wool or woven grasses. Outside, though, were plains and a lake and mountains. If I really stretched my imagination, I could see the exit shelters and com dishes of Ontar far away across the yellow-brown plains. I walked to the nearest window. Beyond and below it, the lake sparkled in the sunlight.

"Take an hour, or two, or three," Ennis said. "Whatever you need, within reason." He retreated to a shabby rug near the door and sat down with his back to the wall. He closed his eyes as if he were going to go to sleep.

"I need to be alone to think," I said.

Ennis opened his eyes and gave me such an eloquent look that he needed to say nothing. He wasn't going to take the slightest chance I'd escape.

I looked out another window at the snowy mountains and wondered if I'd ever see Ontar or Karne again. I boosted myself onto the window's deep sill and started to push open the casement. Ennis leaped from the floor, wrapped his arms around me, and pulled me out of the window faster than I would have believed possible.

"No!" he said harshly. "You aren't escaping. Especially not that way."

Surprise kept me silent for a moment; then I laughed. There was nothing else to do: I'd known too much fear and anger that day. Ennis looked taken aback. His arms loosened slowly and he stepped back.

"Self-murder isn't an out for Halareks," I finally said. "I just wanted to see better."

Ennis looked dubious.

"Truly." I tentatively rested one hand on his arm. I smiled at him even more tentatively. "You can't think the idea of lying with you, even if forced, is so abhorrent that I'd *kill* myself?"

I could almost see the gears in his brain go round. Was he going to feel insulted? Then he grinned, ruefully.

"No, I think better of my skills than that, but if I let you escape, I'll lose equipment essential to enjoying my skill."

It was becoming clearer and clearer to me how Richard kept such control of his people, even from prison. But Ennis was Harlan. What did it matter to me if he were mutilated because I escaped?

It did matter, though. I was helpless, alone among enemies in an isolated location that was essentially immune from suspicion. He hadn't needed to be either courteous or kind to me. Richard would not have been. Nor Brander, either, I was willing to wager.

I let my hand fall to my side. "I won't jump. Self-murder's a disgrace worse even than marrying a Harlan. Just let me smell fresh air for a while and think."

He hesitated, then backed away and resumed his place beside the door. I wished he'd wait outside, but I knew better than to ask. It was trust enough for now that he left me alone beside a window that opened. I climbed back up onto the sill and pushed open the casement. It felt very odd, opening a window. Ontar manor has a few imitation windows (many manor houses do) but they don't open and if they did, they would open onto the stone that encases the house.

The outside air was very sharp, even for Drak. Drak, and then Narn, and Uhl with its storms and the ending of travel until spring. Would I still be here in spring, cooped up all winter with Brander? Pregnant, perhaps, before the first Thaw? Never in my worst dreams had I imagined I could be a stolen bride. Black Ship women, that's who the stolen brides were, women stolen from other worlds. Women on Starker IV had families that would begin feud in their defense, but most nearby worlds, and all the worlds of the Old Empire, had given up war. Five generations past The War was, but that was not nearly long enough to forget its effects. Starker IV, with its cities far beneath the surface, had been impregnable, immune; so Starker IV, Karne said, had not learned a necessary lesson.

The War had, indirectly, brought the Sickness to us. No weapon could reach our cities or manor houses. No weapon except biologics dropped into ventilation shafts. House Kerinnen had thought to gain advantage by doing just that. Its weapon killed so many children among the Houses in the first years that it became a parent's only fear, and it poisoned the genes of all who survived. So it was called the Sickness, and because of it, House Kerinnen had been destroyed to the last stone and pebble and the hole filled in. After the first generation, the Sickness killed only girl children, either at once or by the time they were two. Male children got sick, but they lived and became immune. As a result, women of noble blood soon were in very short supply. Women of the correct rank and Family connections, that is. Of Freewomen there were always plenty.

I stared at the yellow-brown landscape. Ennis could find no woman of blood and had thought to die childless. I had the rank and Family connections. I also had genes Harlan wanted, and Ennis had genes Richard wanted preserved. I was enemy, and therefore a target. I was marriageable. I was *married*. I shut my eyes against tears. There would be no more tears!

That was easier said than accomplished, however. I had to bend my head forward and pinch my nose high up between my eyes to prevent tears from falling. Arl had been a good-hearted and loving man and now he was dead. Dead because of a feud that did not even involve his House.

An icy wind gusted through the window. I looked beyond the end of the lake to the mountains. Cold, hard, unyielding.

Hope, what tatters of it I'd had left, died. This was McNeece land, ally land. I'd never be found here. For the first time, I understood what life was like for Black Ship brides. Mother had never talked about her capture or her first months here. Now it was easy to imagine the pain, terror, humiliation, and reduction from personhood to the status of a baby machine she had experienced. I had experienced all except the pain, and Ennis had promised there would be no pain if I didn't fight him. Other men were not so kind. Where there was pain and terror, it would go on for years, because marriage is for life, except if the wife commits adultery or if she is barren. Ennis would have to die before I could escape Harlan control, and whether I went to him willingly or not made no difference.

On the other hand, I could make coupling so unpleasant he'd—no, Ennis had been kind, but he wasn't soft, and to be here and *not* married would be worse than becoming a Harlan wife. I'd be shamed beyond redemption.

Would Karne accept a marriage-by-Broken-Seal? For a moment doubt swept me. Karne had changed a lot since his return from Balder. He accepted more Gharr customs and rules now. Did that mean he'd accept a forced marriage without a fight?

I slid out of the window and began pacing, the soft-soled boots that had been a wedding present from Lady Agnes shushing against the stone floor. Karne would know how dangerous a child of mine could be if it were half Harlan. If it were a boy, it would be Heir in Halarek if Netta's boys should die and, for Richard, the death of two children would be a slight matter.

I paced and thought for a long time. I'd never before been faced with a problem that had no good solutions. When I stopped at a window and looked out again, the sky was purpling and the taller rocks stretched long black shadows toward the tower. They were dark, blind shadows, forerunners of night. Blind, as I had been. I'd never seen harm in the Black Ships before, except in the tremendous expense. Mother seemed to have accommodated herself to her new life very well, so I'd always seen the Black Ships as a relatively safe way to provide descendants and untainted blood for the Houses.

I wished now that Mother had talked about how it had been for her. Perhaps the fact that she did *not* talk about her coming should have told me something. Perhaps Father had employed an especially effective spy to pick out his wife-to-be. Perhaps Mother had been especially adaptable. Grief came, then tears, as much for what I'd freely given up as for what had happened since. I could've chosen Nik. I could've refused the contract with deVree. It would've been a long fight in both our Houses, but we might have won.

Don't delude yourself, Kathryn Magdelena Alysha Halarek, my mother's spirit scolded. *Neither House can afford a tie with a House already so close.*

I tried to suppress the pain, but it wouldn't stay suppressed. To lie with an enemy for the making of a child, even if that child be Halarek's Heir—

"Oh, Nik," I whispered to the shadows, "we were fools to turn away from love and joy for something as stupid as Family honor and power."

I crumpled into a little heap and cried and cried and cried. It was almost dark by the time I wiped the tears from my face with my palms, smoothed the wrinkles from my dress, and pulled the wedding shawl around my neck into a hood to conceal the puffiness of my face. Brander might have enjoyed exhibiting signs of my tears to the tower's guards. Somehow I knew Ennis wouldn't.

"Feeling follows behavior," my mother had always said. Now I had a chance to find out if that were true. "I'm ready now," I said.

Ennis stood and held out his hand. I took it and he led me to his room.

CHAPTER 4

In return for nonresistance, Ennis gave me more than just escape from pain. He was gentle, unfailingly kind, and very skillful. By the time nightmeal was announced, his bed had a blood-spotted sheet, should Brander have demanded to see it, and I'd learned that the act of marriage can be deeply pleasurable.

Did we look satisfied when we went to dinner? I suspect so, because Brander only gave us an assessing look and motioned us toward the table. Ennis and I would be sharing a long couple's plate, as was the custom for husband and wife. The servants set out the food, and the meal progressed with only occasional talk—a request for a vegetable, perhaps, or to have the wine or brandy passed. I found eating from the same plate as Ennis strangely intimate.

After dinner, Ennis showed me the library and the game cabinet at the back of the room. On Starker IV we know a lot of games, because we're shut away so long each winter. We played a little chess that night, left the game to finish later, and went to bed.

The evenings usually went that way—nightmeal, games or

reading, then to bed. When Ennis or Brander had company, however, from House Harlan or from Odonnel or from the minor Houses that were vassals of one House or the other, I went to sleep alone. I eventually noticed there was never a day without at least one Family man other than Brander present, and that these men always seemed to be of equal rank to Ennis. Was it possible Richard or others in Odonnel or Harlan didn't trust Ennis completely?

Daytime was often boring. There isn't much to do at a hunting lodge if one isn't hunting. Sometimes Ennis took me out riding. It was good to get out in the air, though we were heavily guarded at all times. More frequently, we took long walks, on which we had long talks. These were better than riding, because the guards were fewer and stayed farther away.

As the weeks passed and we got to know each other, Ennis risked teasing me, and bedtime was what he teased me most about. He would invite me to bed by saying it was time to practice; a virgin as I had been needed a *lot* of practice to catch up to him, he would say, always with such seriousness in his face and voice and with such a twinkle in his eye!

Time in bed was never boring. I occasionally thought of the preventatives I had had with me. My dresses had been returned to me and small personal items like perfume and face cream, but the preventatives had not. I don't think I would've used them. A quick pregnancy was important. I'd learned Ennis needed one if he were to keep his position in Harlan. If Ennis didn't succeed with me, some other Harlan male, probably not nearly so gentle or kind, would replace him. Still, I didn't want to raise a child in Harlan. I think Ennis began to understand that. His boyhood had been rougher than Karne's, and he, too, had learned much from a wise and loving mother.

Narn passed. The daytime routine continued. Ennis taught me fencing and otherwise made himself pleasant company during the mornings. The library was large and varied, unusual for a hunting lodge, and enough to fill my afternoons. Then came nightmeal and guests. The food was always good and the servings generous, in the expectation that I'd soon be eating for two, I often thought, rather bitterly. I hated being viewed as a broodmare, which is exactly how the Harlan hierarchy saw me.

After nightmeal, Ennis, Brander, and their guests often withdrew to do whatever men do when they go off by themselves. I would go to the library, select a book, and retire to the upholstered chair in our room. At our customary bedtime, a servant always brought a steaming All Night, whether Ennis was there yet or not. All Nights are always sweet and heavy and supposedly aid sleep. Besides the All Night, Ennis customarily sent me something special when he stayed up with guests—chocolates, a flower, a special book (though there were always guests, he didn't always stay up). The gestures began to mean more to me than I was comfortable with. It wasn't that I loved him, because I didn't. It was that I trusted him and was beginning to care for him and to worry what would happen to him when I finally escaped or was rescued. I still believed I would be rescued, though my hopes had become much more realistic, pinned on a public announcement either of my pregnancy or of the birth of the child, either of which would locate me for Karne.

One morning I awoke to nausea and disorientation. I reached the Sanitary just before my stomach emptied itself. I retched until my stomach was dry, then crumpled onto the cold tile floor. I'd missed one month already, but I'd blamed it on the distress and grief of the massacre. Temporary cessations are natural in such circumstances. I couldn't so explain away the second, not accompanied by sickness as it was. I was carrying Ennis's child.

For the first few moments after that realization, I did, in spite of what I'd told Ennis, think of suicide. Dying had to be better than birthing a baby who would permanently put Halarek under Harlan's hand. But the tower, with its convenient fall onto sharp rocks, had been closed up tightly for two weeks already, and the escape stairs to the surface were always guarded. Besides, self-murder really wasn't a Halarek way out. Halareks didn't give up. They fought until there was no life in them.

After the first despair passed, matters began to look better. Maybe Harlan would loosen its guard once my belly began to expand. Maybe I would even be moved somewhere more civilized for the birth, if the baby was as important to Harlan as Ennis thought. At the very least, there'd be an announcement of the baby's birth. Richard Harlan would not pass up such an opportunity to gloat.

Ennis knew I was pregnant without being told, and his gentleness and tenderness increased. It was during this time, after we'd begun to trust each other, that I learned how our breeding had come about. Ennis wanted to reassure me, I think, by letting me understand what I'd escaped and so value him more. I couldn't have valued him more. He had been far more a friend to me than most women expected even from a marriage into a friendly House.

It seems Richard planned to capture me, sneak me into Breven, use me until I was pregnant, and then send me home. Ennis had to stop for a few minutes right there, because the idea was so horrifying I couldn't listen for a time. The damage such a plan, if successful, could do to a House, to my House, is difficult to explain adequately. For me, the plan meant pain (because Richard wouldn't have prepared me as Ennis had), humiliation, and, finally, ostracism for Gharr society. For my House, it meant degradation, humiliation, isolation, contempt (because it showed the world Karne couldn't protect his sister from the most serious insult possible), and finally political destruction. The present plan applied the same list to Karne, but not as strongly, because many Houses had lost women to competitors and enemies over the generations.

Harlan's vassals wouldn't permit Richard to carry out his plan. *They* had no desire to see Halarek die. If they demanded that Richard refrain, what else could he do? He was confined to Breven. But he had insisted on the kidnapping to show Karne he still had power, even while in Breven. It followed easily then that Harlan's genetic council selected a suitable mate for me from the males in that House and Richard accepted its choice. This was the first time I, or perhaps anyone outside Harlan, had heard of its genetic council. Ennis explained that half the power of his House came from selective breeding. The large number of females that resulted, and the marriages these females made, created important alliances in a female-short market.

"Women are valued in Harlan," he said.

Perhaps this explained in part his gentle treatment of me. Brander, on the other hand, apparently did not extend Harlan's valuing of women to women not of that House. He seemed to sense how my pregnancy increased my hope of rescue, and he taunted me with how a child of Halarek blood would be trained in Harlan ways. He also talked, in elaborate detail, of the traps and ambushes waiting for Karne should he make any attempt to rescue me. The threats left my nerves thrumming with anxiety and fear. I had to warn Karne, somehow, that an attack was expected. I walked the halls of the lodge, often for hours, thinking. My fear for Karne was one of the few things I couldn't talk to Ennis about by that time. There was no possibility of trusting a Harlan with questions about how to warn Halarek about a military trap.

Brander teased and prodded at me with his threats. Since I couldn't assess how much was really threat and how much mental torture, my need to warn Karne and the Family grew stronger and stronger. But no plan came to me, and it was already late in Uhl. There would be no travel, even if I could find a bribable servant. By spring—I tried not to think about spring. The baby was due in the spring, two weeks or more before the Thawtime Council meeting. On the other hand, when no one could travel, Karne and Lizanne and Netta's boys would be safe.

Only Thawtime Council would be too late for a warning. Richard would want this child to be the sole surviving heir by the time of Council. He wouldn't even think of the possibility that my child might die at birth (so many did) or be female. Would his spies in House Durlin kill? All the Houses had spies—spies working for them, spies working against them. . . .

But spies were not assassins, usually.

Then came another blow. Ennis told me, with some trepidation, I think, that we were to be married with all the ceremony of The Way in House Odonnel on 15 Kerensten and that it would be tri-ded all over the world. I must have looked the rage that boiled up in me, because Ennis took a step backward.

"I won't let you be embarrassed," he began. "A seamstress has been hired to make a magnificent dress—"

"Fifteen Kerensten!" I shouted at him. "Fifteen Kerensten! Who thought of that? You? Or your master?"

"Wh-what's the matter? That's First Thaw this year, the New Year, a time of great celebration."

"It's my birthday! I'm to be married to a Harlan in House Odonnel *on my birthday!* Can you think of a better way to demonstrate my brother's weakness?"

"Oh, Lord!" His palm hit the side of his head. "Richard again." He came to me, took my hands, and squeezed them in a way that had always calmed or comforted me. "There's nothing I can do now, even if what I want counted with Richard. It's been announced."

We were in the library. We had agreed to play chess. I sat down beside the board and looked at the pieces. I was feeling like a pawn. So, apparently, was Ennis. He released my hands and turned his back. That usually meant he had something to say he knew I wouldn't like.

"The dress can be any design you like, Kathryn, but it will be the deep blue of your House combined with the green of mine."

I burned with resentment. The dress would be hideous, because of what it represented, no matter what its design, and I would have to wear it in front of the entire Harlan clan plus however many people decided to watch the ceremony on tri-d. I didn't take my resentment out on Ennis. How could I? Not many people could outthink Richard, in the first place, and I knew enough of House politics to know the price he might pay for interfering in Richard's plan, even though in the most important part of that plan, the baby, Ennis had succeeded. The humiliation of a public ceremony, when I would be far gone in pregnancy, and on my birthday—what more vivid proof could there be that the Lharr Karne Halarek could not protect his women?

The insult intended by the wedding and the using of a holy service to give injury—those gave me energy, something I'd had little of for some weeks. I had a date now. I would get a message out somehow, in spite of winter, so Lizanne and her baby and the boys would be protected.

I knew the tri-d room would be guarded. It always was, or I would've used it at once. That was part of what being a tomboy had given me, a way into friendship with tri-d techs and com-techs and even pilots.

I prowled the lodge. I'd already learned on earlier walks how meager a residence it was. The kitchen would hold no more than the cook and two or three helpers. There was no conservatory. The stable area was very small, more for the sheltering of horses that would soon return to their own manors than for the keeping of them. The arena was only large enough to exercise one horse at a time and had no practice dummy: Ennis and I practiced fencing on each other. The servants' quarters were on the fourth level, with the dining hall and tri-d room and the flitter pad, instead of on a level by themselves. There were, of course, no exits except the emergency ones, because there was no city outside the walls to exit to.

I'd never seen many servants—only the cook and her helpers, a groom, two or three cleaners, and Ennis's personal body servant. There was also perhaps a squad or so of soldiers, the techs who ran the tri-d room and the com center, and the seamstress, of course. I had no personal maid, another insult that Ennis had tried to correct, but Richard meant the slight to stick. At least the omission freed me of a probable spy.

At the beginning of Arhast, when the last winter supplies were to come from the Gild, I saw a way to get a message out. The Gild drop would come from a Gildship in orbit and it was a measure of the boredom of my daily routine that I went to watch. The crates, their contents heavily cushioned, fall from the Gildship onto a large platform on the surface. The force of impact sets a switch and causes the platform to descend rapidly.

I arrived just after the platform hit the freight area. Ennis was sleeping in, so I hadn't had to think of an excuse to keep him away. I tugged my cloak tight around me to keep out the dense cold falling down the freight shaft and watched the cook and her helpers haul away foodstuffs. Soldiers unpacked the rest, then stacked the empty crates on the far side of the freight-drop platform. In spring, the platform would be sent to the surface again and the Gild would send a flier for the crates, if there were a lot, or pay a caravan to bring them back if there were only a few. I didn't notice when the surface doors closed.

The crates were sturdy, plasti-form boxes. They would take many such drops from orbit before they needed to be ground up and remade. Someone at the Gild would inspect them before they were reused, though. This I knew from my dealings with the Gild as the mistress of Ontar manor. That person would find a note if I left it carefully.

I walked to the platform and circled it slowly, as if I were figuring out how it worked. The soldiers carrying out the last of the crates looked at me suspiciously, but went on with their work. I reached the stacks of crates and began poking through them.

"Hey!" A soldier put down his crate and sprinted across the room toward me. "Get away from those."

I stiffened to look as powerful as I could and turned to face him. "I'm a daughter of the Nine. Speak to me with respect."

The soldier flushed. "My lady, I didn't know it was you. You aren't dressed like—"

I let myself relax a little. The soldier hadn't slighted me intentionally. It was another small humiliation, that I could not dress to suit my rank. "I'm looking for a little box. I would have sent a servant if I had one."

My small request made a large difference in the soldier's behavior. He almost wiggled with eagerness. "My lady, let me help."

He dug through the top layers of crates. I watched carefully, sometimes setting a crate upright again when his digging dislodged it. In the process, I discovered that most of the crates had heavy foam linings. One or two had linings that were ripped or dented through to the outer slats. One of these was what I needed, a crate that would have to be taken apart and repaired before it could be reused. I could slide a note into a tear where it wouldn't be seen and then pray that it would be found during repair.

"Ha!"

From the satisfaction in that word, I knew the soldier had found something. Whatever it was, it would be acceptable, because I'd found what I needed.

What he carried proudly down the side of the pile was a solid, lidded box. He opened it. It, too, was heavily lined inside with foam. It must have contained something too small for one of the crates, or perhaps too precious.

I put on a beaming smile. "Oh, that's just what I need. Thank you so very much."

The soldier reddened with pleasure, bowed, and went back

to his work. I took the box and hurried to our room. Ennis had gone, thank goodness. I had to write the note quickly, both because Ennis might come back and I didn't want to have to lie to him and because the soldiers might lock up the freight room once the unloading was done.

The freight room was locked when I returned, the note to the Gild tucked tightly into my cuff. I spent more than half an hour convincing the soldier who guarded it that I needed the door opened because the box the prefet had found for me was too small for my purpose and how important a box was to protect the precious book my beloved late mother had given me and . . .

I blithered on until the guard got tired enough of my chatter to check with the prefet, verify my story, and open the door.

A large number of crates had been stuffed into a cargo net, ready to be lifted to the surface. I poked around the pile at the edges, then climbed it, looking for a damaged crate. I could tell from the guard's muttering under his breath that he did not approve of my unladylike scrambling. I had to find more than a crate. I had to find another small box to support my story to the sentry. Almost immediately I found one, somewhat smaller than the first actually, but I looked half an hour more before finding a crate with a lining ripped enough to make hiding the note easy, yet not ripped so much that the note would fall out when the soldiers piled more crates on or when the net was jerked upward. I stashed the note in the rip, piled more crates on top of the one I'd used, and climbed down the pile.

"I've found one!" I cried to the guard, waving my little box over my head and trying to act inordinately thrilled about it. I felt very silly.

Such behavior was apparently just what the guard expected. He looked at me with the semi-bored tolerance such men reserve for flighty women and let me out the door with a small bow.

Later that evening, as I sat sipping an All Night and thinking, I realized how futile that note was. Arhast, Koort, Nemb, Kerensten, then Verdain and the Thawtime Council and the arrival of the baby. I'd let hope run away with reason. The Gild couldn't grab a freight net from the surface at this time of year and it certainly wouldn't send a flier out after one. No one ever flew this time of year. Even Nik, a skilled and dare-devil pilot, had never taken a ship up in Arhast. Bringing the wounded back from Farm 3 late in Uhl had been dangerous enough. My note would sit in the freight room until Kerensten, at least.

I'd had such hope that I could at least save the other heirs. For a while, I fell into deep despair. The All Night finally had its effect, though, and I got a good night's sleep, which renewed my determination to find a way to warn Halarek. I'd explore the lodge even more carefully, level by level.

I told Ennis I needed the exercise that walking the halls gave me and that I'd rather go alone. He let me go without argument. I started methodically at the top level and worked my way down. There was nothing on Level 1 I could use. The emergency stairs led to the surface, of course, but it was Arhast, and people died, even in survival suits, after a few moments on the surface in Arhast. There were no emergency rockets that I could fire, though there should have been some, but even if I'd found and launched one, there would have been no fliers out to see it. Maybe I could use the emergency stair come spring. Or find a rocket.

"In a well-run house, every exit stair has rockets," I found myself muttering as I turned to go down to the next level.

By the time I'd worked my way down to the more obscure areas of Level 4, it was late in the afternoon. Then I heard and felt the pumps. I felt joy, for the first time in months. Pumps meant water and water goes out. I opened door after door until at last one opened onto a flight of stairs leading down into the pump room. The sinuous black flow of the underground river that kept the lodge supplied with water and electricity flowed into the room at one side and out under the wall at the other.

"Thank you, Guardians," I whispered.

I let my forehead rest against the doorjamb for a minute, waiting for the dizziness of relief to go away. Below was a way out, at least for the note. Below was hope of rescue. I looked carefully around. I saw no serfs or technicians tending the pumps, no one cleaning the room, no one testing the water. I stepped onto the landing at the top of the iron stair and stopped, waiting to see if the clang of my weight of the platform brought anyone out to see what was happening. No one came.

I went down as quietly as one can on an iron stair. I inspected the entire pump area carefully. I saw where the water intakes for the lodge were, where the turbine intakes were, where the water flowed out of the turbines and out of the lodge. Karne had ordered all open stretches of Ontar's water supply to be covered over, for the safety of the workers and of any children who might wander in and think swimming in the swift-flowing water would be fun. Such safety precautions were a new idea, though, and considered unmanly by many. I thanked God and the Four Guardians that the river under McNeece's lodge was still open. Then I went back up to our room.

A pen had been among the few personal things returned to me. No paper, just the pen. I searched the room, but there was nothing to write on except the borrowed books. I quickly decided neither paper nor ink would survive the trip I had in mind for the note, anyway. In the end, I used a pillow cover as paper, grease from the remains of the fast-breaking Ennis had ordered in became the ink, and my finger as a pen. I dipped my finger in the grease, stretched the cloth as tight as I could with one hand and several books, and wrote. Nightmeal time approached and I wasn't finished. I wrote as rapidly as possible with such tools and prayed Ennis didn't come up to see what was keeping me. When I finished, I reread the note, then laid it carefully under the bed.

I allowed the grease to soak in for several days, then let the cover lie in klag overnight in the Sanitary (where Ennis was less likely to notice it) to make it brown and the letters easier to read. Early in the morning, after the cloth had dried, I folded it tightly, stuffed it into the smaller of the two padded boxes, ripped the lining from the larger padded box, stuck the small box inside that, tied the outside box tightly shut with one of my cloth belts, then began my now customary pacing of the lodge's hallways. I wore a light cloak against the early morning chill. It also hid the box, which was tucked securely under my arm.

It seemed absurd to turn down the heat for the night as if the lodge cooled off like a surface building would do, but my people have several customs reflecting their former life on the surface of another world. Ontar, city and manor, still set the lights for "day" and "night," for example. Ontar city even had carefully programmed "moonlight," and many Halareks still wore dress cloaks inside, but at least they didn't insist that everyone be uncomfortably cold of a morning because ancient ancestors on another world had been.

On the other hand, I told myself, no one will think it unusual that I'm wearing a warm cloak this morning. I didn't want to think what could happen to me if I were caught sending a message to the "enemy." I did know that if I were discovered, Ennis would be in too much trouble himself to spare any help for me.

No one stopped me. No one even seemed to notice me. I reached the pump room without trouble and slid the box into the powerful flow of water running out of the cooling apparatus and under the lodge wall. I stood looking after it for several minutes after it disappeared, my prayers that it be found by friendly hands in its wake.

CHAPTER 5

Karne strode through the halls toward the flitter pad. Nik was arriving, Uhl or not. He hated meeting him surrounded by guards from the household Blucs, but they were necessary. Kit's kidnapping had made them necessary. Knowing that did not prevent outrage from burning through Karne anyway. The Lharrs Halarek *never* used personal guards. Karne knew of no lord, even in the minor Houses, who had personal bodyguards. Wives, yes. Children— Memories of the rumors and innuendoes and outright insults that had made his life, and the ruling of his House, so difficult during his first year home came back, raw and painful. They could begin again if his enemies learned he had bodyguards. He could die and leave Halarek without heirs if he did *not* have them.

Two of the guards opened the door to the flitter pad and quickly checked the area for intruders. The newly arrived flitter's exhausts glowed pinky red and steamed gently. Its occupant waited until the guards had finished their inspection before he stepped out onto the flitter's wing. Karne strode forward to greet him, consciously keeping himself from running, which would show an unseemly eagerness. The man on the wing hopped to the pad surface.

"Nik!"

"Karne!"

The two men shook hands, laughed, pounded each other on the shoulder, then turned from the flitter and walked back toward the waiting guards.

"Only you'd fly this late in Uhl, Nik." Karne's voice held both concern and admiration.

Nik von Schuss shrugged and looked at the men in deep blue uniforms standing on alert at the edges of the room. "Guards, huh? Things are bad indeed."

"Kit's probably alive and probably being used as a brood mare, so the risk of assassins here is high."

"Assassins in your manor in winter?" Nik's voice was carefully neutral.

"It's happened before," Karne snapped. "To my grandsire's sire."

Nik's hand gripped Karne's shoulder for a moment, then the two men joined the guards by the door. The group took the nearby lift to Level 4. Karne led his friend into the private, personal-family dining room next to the library and sent one of the guards to the kitchen to pick up the late dinner that had been set aside for them.

While they waited for the food, Karne briefed Nik on what had been learned about the kidnapping, little as it was, then added, "The Duke deVree had teams out looking for landing-scorch in unusual places all over this hemisphere, right up to the first of this month, but they found nothing." Karne shook his head. "Arl's loss is a bad blow to that House."

Nik nodded, but absently. "The duke has other sons. Halarek has only you and Kit."

Two pages brought in trays of food. They set the food, plates, and utensils on the table in silent efficiency, then left. The fragrance of klag soon filled the room. Karne and Nik sat down and began to eat.

"There are Kerel's boys," Karne said. Surely Nik had not forgotten the two children in House Durlin.

Nik's mouth twisted up at one corner. "No offense to your

brother meant, but they're not only very young, they're not overly bright.''

Karne sighed. Kerel had not been overly bright, either. ''No offense taken. Netta was pretty and rich, and Kerel had his pick of the market.'' Netta had been and still was astonishingly beautiful, but there were no brains inside her pretty head. Karne felt a twinge of anger and jealousy. He himself had been offered the dregs of the market, and that would not have been different had his sire lived. ''Besides, Kerel wasn't the Heir,'' he added. ''Jerem was. Hereditary stupidity was not so important in Kerel's children. Or so my sire thought.''

''And Jerem produced only girls.''

Karne nodded. ''And they all died of the Sickness.'' Karne's open hand hit the dining table with a loud crack. ''And *my* wife produces no living children at all!''

As if that frustrated, bitter cry had been a summons, Lizanne Arnette, Larga in Halarek, knocked timidly at the slightly open door. Karne wondered guiltily if she had heard his angry outburst. She had been hurt enough before she came to live in Halarek. He didn't want to hurt her more. It wasn't her fault she couldn't carry a child to term. Karne set down his fork and beckoned her in.

''How can I help you, Lizanne?''

Lizanne crossed the room heavily and stood close beside Karne before she would speak. ''My—my sire would speak with you, milord.''

Her voice shook as though Lord Francis still had the power to punish her whenever and however he chose. Karne looked up at her. She had been a bad bargain for the Lharr Halarek, though she had had an excellent dowry. A sign, perhaps, of Lord Francis's eagerness to dispose of this unwanted daughter, that dowry, though it had paid off many of the debts from the war on Harlan.

Karne patted her hand awkwardly. ''You can go back to your room and rest. I'll send Tane to tell Lord Francis I can't speak with him right now.'' He gave her what he hoped was a reassuring look. ''If your sire asks to speak to you again, have your maid tell him I've forbidden you to use the tri-d.''

Lizanne's relief gave a soft glow to her pallid face. ''Thank you, milord,'' she breathed.

Her gratitude for such a small effort to spare her pain embarrassed Karne. "Dr. Othneil says there's only two more months till the baby comes. I don't want you to be frightened or upset again."

"My lord!" she whispered. She snatched his hand from the table and kissed it. "I'm so lucky to have a lord who cares about me." She bowed slightly, a courtesy entirely unnecessary between man and wife, and left the room.

Karne waited until she was well gone, motioned the guard outside to shut the door, then swore softly. "Care about her! Dear God! I protect her as I would an abused dog and she—"

Karne spun away from his friend, clenched his hands, and took deep breaths until he gained control of his face and his feelings.

Nik cleared his throat. "And isn't that caring about her?"

"Not the way she means. She means the way I care for Kit or for my mother or for Emil or you. I can't afford to get emotionally attached to my wife. No lord of a House can." He turned again to his friend. "That's one way in which Lizanne is good for me. There's no chance I'll love her."

"Which is what you said when you asked Uncle Emil to call me home. 'Love in marriage is for Freemen, not the great Houses. Love gives an enemy too much leverage.'"

Karne looked his friend steadily in the eye. "And does it give an enemy leverage?"

Von Schuss's face went hard with his effort to control his emotions. "Yes!"

Karne's mouth twisted ruefully. "Well, I'm not going to say 'I told you so.' It was too late for that years ago." He paused and looked down at the plate in front of him. When he spoke, his voice was low. "I'm using your feelings for leverage, too." He was silent for a time. He looked up. "You're the only other person who has as strong an interest in finding Kit as I have. If you do find her, she's yours."

Von Schuss went white and braced his head in his hands for a moment. "Guardians!" he whispered. "I thought never to hear you say that!"

. . .

Uhl and its vicious storms passed. Then Arhast. Having each other's company made the unbearably long wait of winter confinement more bearable. Karne and Nik speculated endlessly about who the kidnapper was and where Kit was and how to get her back. The longer the kidnapper's silence, the more Karne began to fear Kit was dead, though killing her would be against all customs of the Houses concerning feuds and women. Short-tempered and unreasonable, strung tight with fear for Kit and about Lizanne's pregnancy, raging about being confined for the winter, Karne spared only Lizanne the sharp side of his tongue. Nik was little better. Many days the two of them ended up in the arena, fighting off their fear in duels of various sorts or by racing horses. Karne became very adept at swordplay—something that had been of no use at the Academy on Balder—thanks to hours of fighting the sword-dummy, then polishing his skills against a talented human opponent, Nik. Lizanne, as her birthing time approached, seemed to spend most of her waking hours either reading in her quarters or crying. A single sharp word was enough to send her into fits of tears.

This entire mess is the result of being desperate for an heir, Karne kept telling himself. He tried to make himself believe Lizanne would produce a child this time, but it was hard to do.

On 13 Koort, Lizanne gave birth to a beautiful baby girl with her sire's golden eyes. She was named Alysha, after her grandmother, who had also had golden eyes. She lived only five weeks, then died of the Sickness. Lizanne took to her bed and would not be comforted. Dr. Othneil gave her mood-levelers, but her despair did not significantly lessen and Karne slowly ceased to pay more than ritual visits to her quarters. The loss of the hoped-for heir, even if a girl, was great enough. Karne cursed himself for cowardice, but he could not face Lizanne's despair and his own at the same time.

On 20 Nemb, just at the end of First Day Service, an agitated tri-d tech tapped Karne on the shoulder as he rose from prayer. "Milord Karne, there's an urgent message from Abbess Alba. Secured channel, milord."

Karne hurried to the tri-d room. What can Aunt Alba have

to say that requires a secured channel, he asked himself over and over.

His aunt Alba, her stern face and spare figure emphasized by the gray of her habit, waited for him impatiently. She was sitting behind the heavy desk in her Retreat House office, tapping a stylus rapidly against its edge. She acknowledged Karne's arrival with a curt nod. "Peace be on this House."

"And on yours, peace, Aunt." Had their places been exchanged, Karne would have skipped the ritual greeting.

The abbess lifted what appeared to be a dirty piece of cloth from her desk. "*This* is why I use a secured channel, Karne." She flapped the cloth in his direction, then held it vertical and flat so he could see what appeared to be thick letters written on it. "This jammed our intake pumps last night."

The abbess bent over out of sight for a moment and came up with fragments of wood. "It was in this. It appears to be a Gild shipping box. Two boxes, actually, judging from the different woods, though there wasn't enough of the boxes left after the turbines got through with them to tell. It's a note from Kathryn, Karne."

Karne drew in a sharp breath, mouthed "von Schuss" toward one of the techs, and pointed him out of the room.

The abbess's eyes narrowed. "She's his wife now, Karne. You know that. Even if the marriage is of Sheet and Broken Seal." Her tone became more stern than usual. "That is a legal ceremony, Karne."

The fury her patronizing manner always roused stirred in Karne now. He bit his tongue on it. She was his aunt *and* an official of The Way. "The message, Aunt. I thought you called to give me a message."

Alba looked a little disconcerted. She had apparently expected the fury, which would have allowed her to preach about the virtue of controlling one's temper. That was the way their conversations had always gone before the Academy and he had not spoken to her since.

"It's rather hard to decipher," she said finally, "but here's what we think it says." From a paper lying on the desk the abbess read: "My name is Kathryn Halarek and if my brother Karne tries to rescue me, he will die. I've heard them planning.

"It is now 9 Arhast, as best I can tell. I was wedded to Arl deVree on 27 Drak. All in the wedding procession were killed but me, and I'm here at the hunting lodge of Van McNeece at the edge of the mountains of Zimara, the Sealed bride of Ennis Harlan. I carry his child.''

Karne heard a groan behind him. Alba did, too, and looked up for a moment. ''Young von Schuss,'' she said, and went back to reading.

''House Halarek cannot be inherited by one who is half Harlan. You who find this letter, tell my brother where I am. The baby must not be born into Harlan hands.''

''By the Four Guardians!'' Karne looked at his aunt. ''I knew Richard was involved somehow in her disappearance!''

The abbess looked at him in stern disapproval. ''It was not Richard, Karne. Don't let your prejudices carry you away.''

''Prejudices! By my Mother's Blood—!'' Karne stopped, aware of the futility of arguing with the abbess. He was lucky she had condescended to use a secured channel. Though if ''we'' deciphered the message, its contents would be known very quickly in most of the Houses. Too many noble women wintered in spiritual retreat at such places. ''The Lord be with you,'' Karne said automatically, officially ending the transmission.

''And with your Spirit.'' The abbess motioned with her hand and disappeared.

''She's married! Guardians!'' Nik's voice was raw with pain.

''That's better for her than the alternative.'' Karne thought of the ostracism and public humiliations that were the lot of a raped woman unlucky enough to conceive. Or a woman who had only been raped. Among the worlds of the Federation and the Old Empire, things were very different. Karne told himself he would have smuggled Kit off-planet to live on one of those worlds had she come back unmarried. But he knew he could not have: Kit was the only Halarek still likely to have an heir.

''I would have made her my wife, no matter what!'' Nik's voice was fierce.

So Nik's thoughts had been running along the same line as his, only with a lover's, not a brother's, interest in protecting Kit, and his thoughts had been just as unrealistic. ''And ruined your House,'' Karne said quietly. Karne stared at Nik until the other man looked away.

"Okay," Nik muttered. "As Heir, I couldn't have married her if she'd borne a child outside marriage."

Karne could see the despair of that acknowledgment in the slump of Nik's shoulders and the way his hands hung limply from his arms. All hope of Kit had been taken from him, so soon after he had been told he could have her. Karne shook his head. As much as he loved Kit and Nik both, and in spite of his promise to Nik that he could have her if he found her, Karne knew marriage between them would have been nothing but a disaster. A wife was a bearer of children, a bond between Houses and, if a man was lucky, a political and economic asset as well. They could safely be nothing more. Lovers—lovers were something else altogether. Karne again resolved never to become emotionally involved with a woman.

A little later, in the library with Nik, Orkonan, and Weisman, the librarian, Karne was thinking more clearly. A marriage should be no surprise; the surprise was that it was into House Harlan, when the attack had been by Odonnel soldiers. He would have to set Weisman to digging out whatever information about Ennis Harlan could be found. It was not a familiar name.

A month later, when the pain of little Alysha's death was still almost more than Karne could bear, House Odonnel announced by tri-d that it would broadcast a worldwide message in four hours. For such a message, even Freemen turned on their tri-d's, and announcing the message in advance gave plenty of time for word to spread. Karne, Nik, and all the Halarek cousins who had stayed at Ontar for the winter gathered in the tri-d room at the stated time.

The scene that came onto the tri-d screen showed a wide hall much like Ontar's Great Hall, but without the clerestory windows. Odonnel colors hung from the cross over the dais at the front of the hall and draped over the edges of balconies along both sides. Harlan's green flag made a backdrop for a white fur carpet in the center of the dais. Hundreds of people in bright party clothes swayed and murmured on the floor of the hall.

After a fanfare of trumpets and a pair of tumblers in Odonnel checks, who did handsprings across the dais, Garren Odonnel strode to the center of the fur rug. Reddish highlights glinted in his dark brown hair. He looked out over the crowd in his own hall to the assumed crowds in tri-d rooms all over Starker IV. He cleared his throat and flipped his forelock out of his eyes with a toss of his head.

"Lords and ladies, Freemen, servants of this House, I, the Lharr Garren Odonnel, announce to you the approaching marriage of my cousin, Ennis Harlan, to the beautiful Kathryn Magdelena Alysha Halarek."

There was a gasp in the Halarek tri-d room and a roar that was almost a jeer in House Odonnel. Odonnel motioned and a chunky man nearing thirty stepped onto the platform. The man then turned and assisted the woman who followed him onto the dais. She was heavily pregnant. She swayed and seemed about to fall. The chunky man put an arm protectively around her, then the couple turned to face the Lharr Odonnel and the tri-d cameras. Nik swore feelingly and at length.

Odonnel kissed Ennis Harlan ritually on both cheeks as his overlord. Ennis passed the kisses to Kit, who shut her eyes and swayed and leaned her head against his shoulder. Ennis rubbed the back of her neck in what looked like a tender gesture, whispered in her ear, kissed her mouth, and led her from the dais.

Tane Orkonan, in a back corner of the tri-d room, said a word that would have made Pastor Jarvis turn purple.

Odonnel smoothed an imaginary wrinkle from his tunic. "The happy couple will be married on New Year's Day, 15 Kerensten. All members of the Nine Families and the heads of the minor Houses are invited here for the ceremony. We'll have a New Year's party afterward, the like of which no one on this world has ever seen. The Lord be with you."

And the picture was gone. Karne stood in stunned silence for a moment. "Kit's birthday," he said finally. "Her husband, or his master, has set the wedding for Kit's birthday!"

"How better to show her how little her feelings mean?" Nik put in, his tone hard and bitter.

"It sounds like Richard's work to me," Orkonan put in. "Attacking the procession with Odonnel men when she was to marry a Harlan is the same line of thought."

"The wedding's our chance to get her back," Karne said,

"or at least to arrange for a chance." He turned to leave the room. "Find yourself some wedding-guest clothes, Nik. We're going to get safe-conducts from Council and go to a wedding in Odonnel."

CHAPTER 6

Karne led Nik to the Lharr's quarters, immediately flipped up the top of the rok-hide chest at the foot of his bed, and began reeling out clothes.

"What would you like, Nik? Halarek blue? White? Gold? Sorry I don't have anything the right color brown for a von Schuss—"

Nik grabbed Karne's arm and jerked him away from the trunk. "Karne! Wake up! Surely you're not fool enough to trust a safe-conduct into Odonnel, are you? Even if you can get one."

Karne pulled his arm free and glared at Nik. "What's the matter? This is our chance to get her back."

Nik gripped Karne's shoulders and shook him once, hard. "Think, Karne! She's already his *wife*, by Sheet and Broken Seal, just as your aunt said. A formal wedding only makes her his wife in the eyes of the Church. Odonnel's not going to leave the slightest opportunity for Halarek to get her back. She'll be guarded every moment." Nik's fingers tightened until Karne flinched from the pain. "The entire setup—announcement, ceremony, huge party—may be a trap set just for you."

The wild excitement faded. Karne shuddered. He had talked to Nik about the fatality of letting feelings get involved in Family business and here he was, acting like a fool himself. He ran a hand through his hair. "Guardians! What came over me?"

"You love her." Nik turned away and stood very still and very taut.

Karne tried to imagine what Nik was feeling. As Heir in von Schuss he, too, was invited to the wedding, invited to watch the woman he loved married to a man who had raped her and gotten her with child. Nik had to be suffering the pain of the damned, yet he was cooler, on the outside at least, than Karne himself, and Karne had prided himself on his control.

Karne turned and slowly put the clothes back into the trunk. He thought he had reaccustomed himself to the roughness of life on Starker IV, but this wedding he could not pass off as just another Gharr custom. The invitation had been devised as a kind of emotional and mental torture for Halarek at the very least. If Nik were right, it was also intended to be the death of Halarek. Pray the Guardians Harlan and Odonnel had not guessed Nik's involvement with Kit. Then Karne remembered the stricken look on Lizanne's face when he rushed out of the tri-d room. Little Alysha was only a week dead. Propriety demanded six months mourning.

He sank onto the edge of his bed and buried his head in his hands. He spoke slowly. "What could I have been thinking of? Halarek must send regrets. We'll be in official mourning until Drak."

There was a long silence. "But this is too good an opportunity to pass up," he said finally. "I need to see Kit. She's right about not permitting any child with Halarek blood to be raised in Harlan." Karne raised his head but did not look at his friend. "We can go as Freemen, perhaps. Aldermen of York or Londor or . . ."

Nik snorted. "Don't be a fool! How can you escape detection when only you and Kit in all this world have the Larga Alysha's golden eyes?" Nik's voice rose in exasperation and anger. "You'd be exposed for who you are in a moment!"

Nik's criticism stung. Apparently he doesn't trust my judgment in this matter at all, Karne thought. And to think I had a reputation at the Academy for my ability to stay calm and make rational judgments in frightening situations.

Karne did not like his revised image of himself. "I'm not suicidal!" he said sharply.

He lifted the lid of the trunk again and took a small box from one of the latched drawers in the lid. From the box he took two small bottles of clear liquid, each with a transparent brown hemisphere floating in it. "Remember the first Council we attended, the one we had to steal a Harlan flier to get to?"

Nik nodded.

"Someone there accused me of being an impostor because off-world anyone can buy lenses to change the color of their eyes. I hadn't done that, of course. I hadn't even thought of it, but I thought of it later and had a Gildmed prescribe and order a pair for me, just in case I needed them." He stared into the liquid. "Sometime, I thought, it might be useful to lose 'that Halarek woman's' eyes," he murmured, "and Gildmeds reveal no one's business."

He looked up to see some of the tension leaving Nik's face, replaced by hope. After a moment Nik said thoughtfully, "Disguise might be more dangerous than a safe-conduct if we're discovered, Karne."

"Can anything be more dangerous than to be Halarek in Odonnel?"

"Being Halarek in Harlan?"

Karne gave Nik the weak smile his remark deserved and the two of them sat down on the floor beside the trunk to discover what ideas the tangle of clothing and ceremonial objects inside gave them. But Nik's remark made Karne uneasy. Kit already was a Halarek in Harlan and in terrible danger the moment the child was born. This whole disaster could well be Richard's plan. Confinement in Breven did not stop his sharp mind from working and probably not his plotting, either.

Kit needed some kind of protection. A bodyguard would not be permitted, not made up from soldiers of *her* House, at least. But she was alone in terrible circumstances. Karne's thoughts swirled—wedding, rape, birthday, guard, support—and out of the muddle came the image of Lady Agnes. "Nurse" to Halarek children, chaperon, dragonlady, known throughout the hemisphere for her rigid propriety and ethics, Lady Agnes might seem to the Nine an excellent, and safe, attendant for a young woman of the Families. Lady Agnes also had some skills as a midwife. She often attended those ladies of the Nine who did not want a serf woman, or even a Freewoman, in attendance at the birth of their noble children. *If* Kit's captors permitted anyone from Kit's former life to be with her, it would be Lady Agnes. Her mind was sharp, her manner daunting. Lady Agnes would never consent to carry a message out of Odonnel, let alone consider helping Kit escape her legal husband, or so Odonnel and the rest of the world would think. Lady Agnes's intense loyalty to Halarek had not been exhibited outside that House.

Karne realized he was just sitting with his hands in his lap about the same time Nik nudged him, concerned.

"Karne, what's the matter?"

"Kit. She needs protection. I'm trying to work something out. I'll let you know." He returned to lifting items of clothing from the trunk and examining them for potential usefulness.

In the end, Nik and Karne decided that to go as aldermen was the best disguise. Karne sent Tane Orkonan into Ontar to buy appropriate sarks and hosen for both of them. When Tane returned he had also acquired, through contacts of his own, counterfeits of the necklaces worn by aldermen in York and Lews as well as clothes in the correct colors. Karne complimented him strongly. York leaned toward Kingsland, true, but it was in the eastern hemisphere, far from Odonnel Holding. It was unlikely the Odonnels would recognize a Freeman from so far away, and it would be easy to stay out of the way of anyone wearing Kingsland's purple. Lews lay between the Great Swamp and the great central plains and owed obligation for protection to von Schuss. Neither city was likely to send many, or perhaps any, representatives to a Harlan/ Odonnel wedding.

Karne decided to offer Kit and Ennis Lady Agnes's services as companion and midwife as a wedding gift. He knew presenting the lady that way would make refusing the gift difficult, since each wedding gift from the Houses was traditionally announced after a wedding feast by an officer of the House giving the gift. He would send Weisman, a useful but not irreplaceable man, to Odonnel with the announcement.

Those plans made, he stewed and planned and waited as impatiently as a child for New Year's Day. Nik made plans of his own. He let his hair grow and did not shave his mustache, because Freemen preferred a hairy look. Soon he did not look like himself at all. Karne could not risk such changes in his appearance, because of the spy in the manor house. The lenses and freecity colors would have to be enough, and the lenses would be put in only after he was in a flier and about to land.

On the day of departure, Tane carried their carefully wrapped disguises out to the flier, because Karne dared not trust the job to a servant. They would have to rent other fliers at Gildport, since they could not arrive at Odonnel Holding in Halarek fliers and pretend to be aldermen from freecities at the same time.

Karne took the flier's controls. Nik changed into the Lews alderman's clothes after the craft was airborne, then sat in tense silence until they reached Gildport. At every step, from the purchase of Freemen's clothes to the eventual flight home from Odonnel, there was a chance of betrayal, even by the Gild, whose rules of neutrality sometimes made no sense to outsiders. Would the Gild tell anyone that the Lharr Halarek had come to Gildport with a townsman? That they had left separately in rented fliers? Karne and Nik had discussed Karne's arriving disguised, too, but that would have drawn attention to the Halarek flier, and even the Gildsmen would have asked questions, such as, what are two Freemen doing with a Halarek flier, when the Lharr was overlord to neither?

All Karne's worrying turned out to be needless. They acquired two flitters without difficulty and lifted off for Odonnel. Karne changed his clothes quickly, but left the lenses for last, because he could not wear them more than eight hours at a time. They flew in silence. Neither of them had ever been in Odonnel, so no planning could be done beyond their landing arrangements. Worse, what they wanted most to talk about could not be discussed over the open channels of rented fliers.

They approached the borders of Odonnel from very different directions, as aldermen from such far-apart cities must. If they met other aldermen from Lews or York, what would they do? What would a Freemen do if he discovered the masquerade? Karne could not imagine. He could imagine, all too easily, what Odonnel would do to him if his true identity were discovered.

The automatic hailer from von Schuss Holding roused Karne briefly from his thoughts. His flier, just as automatically, identified itself as a Gild rental. Karne altered course so the flier would come over the rest of the holdings from the northeast, then went back to his circling worries. Kit could not be rescued now, because Odonnel was surely counting on a rescue attempt, even after House Halarek had sent its regrets, and would be prepared for it. Odonnel knew that once Kit was married by the Church, all of Council would recognize the marriage as legal and permanent. Karne could kidnap her back, but the entire Council, including the Freemen—who were usually extremely reluctant to interfere in "Family" matters—would support any attempt to take her back to her legal husband. The Freemen recognized the bonds of the Church, if not the older ceremony. And the child was half Harlan and therefore a Harlan dependent, no matter where it was raised.

Karne forced himself toward more cheerful thoughts. He and Nik could learn important things at the parties after the ceremony. If they were very careful and very lucky, one of them might get a chance to talk to Kit, but talk was all there could be. Karne looked down at the soggy landscape, the snow gray with blown dirt and pocked with thaw holes. Perhaps he or Nik could see a way to rescue Kit later, if the baby died. So many did. Suddenly Karne hurt, thinking of that. Little Alysha's few days had been so full of pain.

A hail from Jura came then, followed in quick succession by Emmen, Harlan, and Kath. Karne felt a momentary inner tightening when he heard the Harlan call, but then reminded himself this was a Gild rental and no one ever so much as irritated the Gild. An outright attack was out of the question, even if House Harlan suspected who was on board.

You're letting suspicion drive you crazy! Karne told himself. The Gild is absolutely neutral in Gharr politics. It has no reason to talk to Harlan about rentals and would not answer questions about them from Harlan if asked. Get yourself together. Odonnel's next.

The Odonnel hail came. Karne looked down. The thaw had progressed far enough here near the coast that the tall, rough grasses and reeds of the swamp around the freecity of Londor poked up through the snow. This made the whole area look prickly and brown. In a few moments more, the com dishes of Odonnel Holding and Odonnel manor appeared below. Karne leaned toward the com set, identified himself as Alderman Karsch of York, and asked for landing instructions.

House Odonnel was crowded and noisy. Of the few people Karne recognized, most were Odonnel or Harlan dependents, allies, or vassals. There were very few Freemen, and Karne saw none in the gray and orange of the freecity of York. There were dozens of soldiers, however. Soldiers patrolled the halls. Soldiers guarded doors and stairwells. Soldiers checked identifications at random. Heart in his mouth, Karne hung toward the center of the crowd, out of easy reach, and watched carefully. The soldiers never checked Freemen, perhaps because Freemen wore their city's colors and either a badge or a necklace of office. Perhaps Freemen wore their colors to prevent such searches. Perhaps Odonnel did not want to antagonize any Freemen.

Karne shook his head, thinking of that. The Freemen's sudden and unexpected seizure of the chairmanship of Council three years before still intimidated the Nine. The Freemen and minor Houses held two thirds of Council's votes and they had united then for the first time. Frem Gashen had quite literally dumped the Marquis of Gormsby from the chairman's seat onto the floor. The memory made Karne smile. Once, at least, a Harlan partisan had gotten his comeuppance.

When nearly an hour's watching seemed to confirm that Freemen really were exempt from identification checks, Karne moved out of the crowd to present himself officially to the manor secretary. This, too, was a hazardous step.

The receiving line was long and the secretary exhausted by the time Karne's turn came. The secretary did not even look up from his lists and piles of keys. Karne's official reception consisted of the slap of a room key into his hand and a motion toward the row of servants who showed guests to their rooms. Karne followed the servant automatically, his mind preoccupied with his tired feet, aching back, and his anger at a system that kept people standing so long. The Nine never waited in lines.

A part of him stood aside, listening to the anger. *You're becoming just like them*, it said. *You resolved when you came home to survive without becoming like them. Listen to yourself now! Serfs, servants, even Freemen, stand in lines in your House frequently. For food, for instance.*

Karne's roommates were already settled in, official envoys from the freecities of Leeds, Loch, and Frieden. Servants brought in a hot supper, which was, after introductions, eaten in weary silence. The three men showed no suspicion of his disguise, so Karne assured himself it was successful. It had to continue to be successful or Halarek was doomed.

He did not sleep well. His conscience nagged him about adopting the same arrogance he objected to in the rest of the Nine. More important, his only sister was to be married to an enemy in the morning. She would be married in front of a crowd of enemies, and he could do no more than watch. Odonnel was tempting Halarek and its allies to try a rescue.

I've shown them I can lead an army to victory. I've shown them I can control and increase the power of my House, but they still see me through my sire's eyes—a weakling and a fool! Garren Odonnel was looking forward to a good laugh at my expense. I wonder how he feels now it's clear Karne Halarek really isn't coming.

Karne tossed and fidgeted. His thoughts raced around inside his head without mercy. What would happen to Kit after the ceremony? Would she and Ennis live here or in Harlan? How could he free her? Whether she was married or not, he had to free her. The thought of a nephew who was half Harlan was bad enough. Worse was the possibility that once the child was born and seemed likely to live, Kit would no longer be useful and would be killed, though that would break all the rules.

The call for all guests to assemble in the Great Hall came early in the morning. Karne prepared for the ceremony slowly with limbs that felt weighted with lead. Had Kit been subdued enough that she would stand willingly before the guests and take her vows? Would Ennis or his overlord force them from her? It had happened before, the forcing of vows from an unwilling woman. There were too few women to allow any to refuse an alliance on whim.

Karne walked slowly toward the Hall, his feet heavy and

unwilling. Most of the guests were already milling around inside by the time he arrived, but Nik was waiting, leaning against a pillar in the corridor. A short, round man, also wearing light brown and yellow and the necklace of an alderman of Lews, stood next to him.

Karne thought his heart would stop. Nik had been found out. Karne took a deep, slow breath and swallowed hard. They had played the odds and lost. Was Nik being watched now, so that the minute Karne showed he recognized him, both would be taken?

Karne looked around carefully. No one was watching, at least not obviously. Nik met his eyes and gave no sign that there was trouble. Or had he been warned not to? Karne cursed the suspicion that was all that kept a lord of the Nine alive, took another deep breath, and approached the pair.

The short man bobbed his head politely. "Peace be on you, Karsch of York," he said.

Karne glanced at Nik, who shook his head. "And on you, Alderman . . . ?" *The man's not a danger, according to Nik, but he has to know Nik's a fake.*

"Duval. Klarence Duval."

"Also of Lews, obviously," Karne added.

The man nodded.

Nik motioned the two into the Hall ahead of him. "Let's introduce ourselves better in a side room after the ceremony." As Karne passed, Nik whispered in his ear, "It's okay, at least for now. Explain after."

The Great Hall dripped banners and streamers and reeked of incense and close-packed bodies. Someone's hawk had been released, and it soared and swooped near the ceiling several levels above the floor. Here a dog yapped and over there another snarled. The crowd shifted and murmured and watched the front of the hall expectantly. Ennis Harlan already stood on the white-carpeted dais under the huge wooden cross, trying to look calm. Behind his back, which was easily visible from the Freemen's section in a gallery under the balcony, his hands alternately twisted and clenched.

A blare of trumpets announced the arrival of the bride. All heads turned. Kit entered the Hall through the main door on the arm of Garren Odonnel. She wore a full green gown—

Harlan color—with a long, apparently heavy train. The color was a bad sign. Karne shook his head. Kit walked slowly and unsteadily. At first, Karne thought that was from the train or perhaps from the weight of the tall, conical hat perched in the crown of braids on top of her head. When the pair passed, Karne saw that Kit's eyes were dilated and glazed.

She's drugged! The idea outraged him. *Kit's been drugged so she'd go through the ceremony for them!*

Just then Odonnel and Kit passed the section of the floor reserved for the Nine. Odonnel let his eyes glide over the section slowly.

Seeing if Halarek came, but too late to be in the secretary's report, are you, Garren? Karne felt a small twinge of satisfaction. *He really expected me to come! Garren or Richard or Ennis ordered her drugged because someone really expected me to come and didn't want Kit in any condition to help in her own rescue!*

That was a more reasonable explanation: Garren or Richard or Ennis must have ordered her drugged, because someone had expected Karne to come and didn't want Kit to be able to help in her own rescue. That was a better explanation than the first one. Everyone knew how bad drugs were for unborn babies, so it would likely have taken more than the possibility of Kit refusing to take her vows to cause drugging. Vows could be forced.

As the couple reached the head of the Hall, Odonnel's pastor of The Way stepped onto the dais from the side. Karne had often wondered how a leader in The Way could bring himself to participate in such a travesty. But it happened so often that Karne often imagined a completely Gharr-trained person would not even notice the conflict between what was preached on First Day and what was actually done.

It's because I've lived away, he thought. The path of the Old Gods on Balder is very different, but at least its gods are honest. Their words and their actions match.

Odonnel could not get Kit up the steps by himself, bulky and unsteady as she was. Ennis had to help pull her up to the white carpeted dais. She stumbled on the carpet, falling against the Harlan man. Karne thought he saw surprise and then concern cross Ennis Harlan's face, but decided that wasn't possible. The man was Harlan and had taken Kit against her will. But then Ennis threw Odonnel a sidelong glance that would have meant death to any but an overlord, and that look did not fit Karne's understanding of the situation. Was Ennis surprised that Kit had been drugged? It looked that way.

The pastor muttered the words of the ceremony at a great rate. Ennis answered. Neither could be heard at the fringe of the crowd where Karne stood. That did not matter. Kit and Ennis Harlan had been married for some time already except in the eyes of the Church. Karne began inching toward the end of the dais. Between the ceremony and the feast that followed, Kit would be brought to a nook on the main floor, where ladies-in-waiting would remove her tall hat. He had to get close enough to assure himself she was at least physically healthy. Nik followed him, though not as if they were together.

The pastor turned to Kit. Karne stopped. Kit swayed and looked as if she were about to fold up on the floor. Ennis pulled her close against his side. Kit seemed to be having difficulty saying or remembering the necessary words, because the pastor stopped again and again in his reading, waited, said something, waited, went on. Ennis's face looked tight and angry.

"He hits her, he's dead!" Nik's voice, suddenly behind Karne's ear, was not less savage for its quietness.

Karne shook his head and turned so Nik could see the finger he laid against his lips. Such remarks could get them killed. In addition, after the look he had seen Ennis give Odonnel, he could no longer be sure Ennis's anger was directed at Kit.

But Nik's savage words made clear what would have to happen. Somehow, after the baby was safely born, Ennis had to die. Kit, even if rescued, could not stay in Halarek if her husband were still alive. A husband had total power over a wife and Council would force Halarek, with sanctions or export embargoes if necessary, to give her back. No one—not brother, father, or other relative—had any right to interfere once a woman married. Ennis Harlan, whatever his true role in this plan of Richard's, must die.

Karne glanced toward the dais. The pastor wrapped his

shawl around the couple's joined hands, blessed them, touched each forehead with oil, then unwrapped the shawl. The ceremony was over. Waiting-women were leading Kit away, but off to the opposite side. Karne would not be able to get close to her before Odonnel servants herded all the guests out of the Hall so tables could be set up. Already most of the Freemen around him had moved closer to an exit, and the Odonnel seneschal was approaching. They could risk no disturbance. Karne turned to leave. Nik was no longer behind him. Karne looked over the room quickly. Nik's yellow and brown coat was easy to spot, since most of the Freemen were crowding out the nearest exit. Nik was sliding around columns and in and out among the guests that were left, working his way toward the spot where Kit had disappeared.

"It would perhaps be best if we left as requested and did not watch Alderman Yrt."

Karne started in spite of himself at the voice beside his elbow. Councilman Duval's dark eyes held a warning, so Karne said nothing, but followed the motions of the seneschal and left the Hall, the councilman right on his heels. Once outside, the councilman took the lead. Perhaps fifty meters down the corridor, he opened a door into a small room that looked like a study or library. He seated himself in a deep leather chair and looked up at Karne.

"Sit. Your friend will meet us when he's done what he feels he must do."

Karne sat, every nerve on edge. Nik was at least going to look at Kit from close range. That was dangerous enough, considering his House. What if he attempted to talk to her? What plausible excuse could a Freeman have for talking to a noble lady? Especially on her wedding day? Would Kit recognize him? Could she conceal it, drugged as she was? Karne wished he could have stopped Nik, but pushing through the crowd to catch up would have made both of them very noticeable. He turned his thoughts away from disasters that could happen. Nik would be careful. Karne had to hope that, even in love, Nik would be careful.

Karne looked again at the sturdy merchant in the leather chair. How much did this Freeman know, and what was he going to do with his knowledge? Just a word to Garren Odonnel and he, Karne, would be dead. How could he start a conversation that would let him assess how much danger this man from Lews was going to be? Guardians! Why did Nik *have* to be room comrade of a councilman from Lews?

"Relax, young sir." The councilman's voice was soothing. "My daughter is of an age with your sister."

Karne went icy with fear. Nik had told Duval who they were. When unmasked, Nik had told all!

". . . She'll be much interested in the details of—" Duval stopped abruptly and stared at Karne. His eyes narrowed, he jerked his head back toward the bookcases, and his lips shaped the word *bugs*. "I've presumed too much, Freeman Karsch. Just because Alderman Yrt is a friend doesn't mean I can assume that you and I are on the same footing, though he's told me much about you and your family. Forgive me, please, for talking to you as informally as I would have to Haakon, but he asked me to entertain you while he presents a small gift from Lews to the Lady Kathryn. Perhaps Magdelena— is Magdelena the right name?—can discuss her wedding dress and how she made it with Adrian in person some time?"

Karne gathered his wits. *They've talked enough to invent a first name for Alderman Yrt. And Duval realizes to mention "sister" can be a disaster if whoever listens draws the correct conclusions, so he emphasizes the sister part to draw attention away from it and uses one of Kit's middle names to make clear to me that he knows who I am.* "I'll see what Mag thinks of the idea. I can't promise, of course, but a social contact in another city—"

"I wasn't thinking solely of business, young sir." The alderman hitched up the front of his embroidered ceremonial tabard as he spoke and pulled a pad and stylus from underneath. He began to write, still talking. "We've been introduced, you remember, but barely. Haakon has spoken often of you, however, so I feel I know you." The look that came with this remark was meant for the Lharr Halarek and not the York merchant. "I have two daughters and a son and my trade is fine fabrics for clothing and furniture." He handed Karne the pad.

Karne skimmed it quickly. Too long a pause might make a listener think about notes. "My Adrian is just the Lady Kathryn's age. I won't betray you. Young von Schuss didn't, either. I guessed that if he were here, you would be, too."

Karne looked at Duval, letting his relief show in his face, and handed the pad back. "I'm a horse breeder myself." *At least I can talk about that as if I were in the business, if I have to.* "Haakon knows someone who knows someone in House Odonnel is how we got invited at all. I've never seen such luxury! Perhaps I can stir up some business later tonight, after the feast."

"Perhaps." Duval handed him the pad. "Since you're so young and this is your first time at a wedding of the Nine, I'll presume to tell you that there's a very thin line between social-business dealings at such an affair and pushing."

The pad said: "There are several things you must know and this is no place to discuss them. 'Haakon' and I agreed to meet in the pool after the party tomorrow. Please come."

The door opened. Karne tensed. His hand moved toward the stunner holster that, as a Freeman, he did not wear. It was Nik. He forced himself to relax again.

"Tables are all ready. Food's out. Time to eat." Nik's voice was cheerful, but his eyes were shadowed and his shoulders sagged. He opened his mouth to say more, glanced around the room, and shut his mouth again.

He suspects bugs, too, Karne thought, *and he's learned something that hurts.*

The three men returned to the Great Hall and sat at a table for Freemen. Everyone introduced himself and then the beer and ale were passed. Then came the food, twenty courses over four hours' time. Food from exotic places. Food in strange shapes. Food out of season.

After the food came the gift announcements, which Karne paid attention to only during Weisman's presentation and Odonnel's murmurings about living arrangements, order of precedence among Kit's ladies-in-waiting and he would consult with his seneschal about these matters. House Odonnel came out looking over-cautious and niggardly besides. After the gifts came the entertainment—jugglers, dancers, acrobats, a magician, singers (both solo and chorus), a dog act, a horse act, then more jugglers, dancers (erotic this time), and acrobats. As the drinking and performing went on, the crowd became noisier and more unruly. When the knife fights began, Karne and Nik and Councilman Duval left. They separated outside the Hall door, agreed on the details of leaving the morrow's party early, and went to their rooms.

CHAPTER 7

One of my attendants pushed a stool toward me, but I couldn't locate it well enough to sit on it without help. My head ached, my neck felt compressed from the weight of that cursed bridal hat, the entire scene in the Great Hall looked a little out of focus, and my brain moved with frightening slowness. Someone lifted the great weight from my head. Someone else let down the tight braids, brushed them out, coiled the hair loosely at my nape. One of the attendants whispered a summary of the next events and I couldn't even remember her name, let alone the list. It was not just my eyes that were out of focus. My mind seemed to be out of focus. Events seemed to slip away only seconds after they happened. The crowd. The noise. The fancy clothes. The heavy, dizzying smell of incense. What was I doing here?

The wedding. Richard had insisted on a public and publicized wedding. Or Brander had. I couldn't be sure which now. Maybe I'd never been sure. The wedding to make my possession public. The wedding that might trap Karne in Odonnel. And drugs. Ennis had argued and argued about drugs. He fought Brander.

66

Did no good. Harlan didn't trust me. Or didn't trust Ennis. Or . . .

I struggled to think clearly. Karne. Something about Karne was important. I shook my head, but that didn't clear away the fog inside. The fog stayed and pain came to join it. Drugs. That's why I couldn't think straight. Men had held Ennis so Brander could shoot me full of drugs. But the effects must be weakening. I'd followed a single thought for almost half a minute. I mustn't show it, though. Anger ran through me, but so weakly it took me seconds to recognize it. The baby. Did their drug hurt the baby?

I put my hand on my belly, or intended to. The hand moved as if made of marble. One of the attendants stepped forward and set the hand on the bulge in my lap. On what once had been a lap. I felt nothing move for what seemed like forever. The baby *had* been moving. Yesterday it had been moving. Then something brushed under my palm. Relief. The little swimmer yet lived. I must protect the baby. But the baby was important to Ennis, too. He'd said he wanted children. I'd seen pictures of him with his nieces and nephews. Those looked like he enjoyed children. I could trust Ennis. In all Harlan and Odonnel, I could trust Ennis.

A motion behind my attendants drew my eyes. A man, his hand still sinking slowly toward his side, was watching me intently. He wore the colors of the freecity of Lews. Did I know anyone in Lews? Did anyone in Lews know me? Had he waved to me? To someone else? He looked familiar. And he was willing me to look at him. I could feel it. Only . . .

I opened my mouth to ask an attendant to bring the man closer, but he gave his head an abrupt jerk that meant "don't." The movement, too, was familiar. Nik? It couldn't be. This was an alderman from Lews. I just saw Nik because of the drugs and because I wished the baby were his. The man's mouth formed the words "I love you," then he turned and slipped away through the thinning crowd.

I struggled with the drug fog then. It *was* Nik! Long hair, mustache, Freeman's clothes—it was still Nik! I stopped myself from going after him just in time. As if I could've walked unsupported any distance. Damn Richard Harlan! I'd almost betrayed Nik, and probably Karne, too.

I shut my eyes to prevent my ladies from seeing any change in them. Nik was here, Karne probably was, too, just as Brander had planned. Only they were disguised. *Think, Kathryn*! But no amount of mental shouting could erase the numbness of the drugs. In fact, the effort of trying to think coherently caused me to feel very tired and disoriented.

Shortly after Nik disappeared, my attendants helped me off the stool and onto the dais for the wedding feast. I spent the rest of the evening at Ennis's side. I could only pick at the food. I was too tired from fighting the drugs and too sick with worry to eat, too disoriented to excuse myself and leave. I examined all the tables in the Hall one by one. It took so long and required such concentration that I didn't find the table set aside for Freemen until after the acrobats had finished their performance and were scrambling for the coins tossed to them. As I watched, three Freemen stood and left the room, two from Lews and one from York. If one from Lews was Nik, was the other Karne? No, that would be too obvious and, besides, he was too short and too stout. The alderman from York, then? He was of a height and thinness with Karne. . . .

I let my head fall against the deep carvings on the back of my chair. It could make no difference. I wouldn't see Nik again. Whatever they had come for, it was not rescue. I was too heavily guarded. The entire manor was too heavily guarded. And I was now married, in the eyes of men and of God.

When I awakened in the morning, the room came into focus immediately, which was somewhat surprising. I'd felt so awful I'd left the feast before it ended, a serious breach of etiquette. Ennis still slept, one arm over my hip, his head turned away. He had come to bed with me last night. It was custom, even though I obviously had had my "wedding night" some months ago. There was no more need for drugs. I was tied to Harlan as tightly as law and religion allowed.

I sat up slowly and let my feet hang over the side of the bed. It was hard, still, to get used to dressing myself, taking care of my clothes myself. What there were of them that still fit. All my life a maid had been waiting with warmed slippers for my feet and a robe to put over my nightdress the moment I awoke. A maid had brushed the dust or wrinkles from my dresses, polished my shoes, brushed and braided my hair. I sighed and stood. The chill of the floor made my toes curl. I resolved that if I ever had a manor of my own, I'd never, ever allow the heat to be turned down at night.

Someone had come in during the night and laid out a party dress. It was bad enough having to dress and groom myself. To have to wear garments that looked like tents was the crowning blow. I sighed again and began the long process of getting myself ready for the all-day festivities. When it came time to button the dress, I had to wake Ennis. There was no way I could reach all the buttons. He did them up for me and then went back to sleep. I envied him his man's short dressing time. *His* body servant wouldn't come for at least another hour.

I had plenty of time to think while I brushed the tangles from my hair. Defiantly, I braided it afterward into a thick cord that hung over my shoulder, a braid such as a woman would wear for supervising the cleaning or for tending the sick. If Richard wanted fancy, he should have given me a waiting-woman who knew how to do fancy! I would do something more elaborate only if Ennis asked me to, and I suspected my small rebellion would suit him just fine, a small retaliation for the drugs of yesterday.

Thinking of waiting-women made me think of Lady Agnes, who had always supervised my waiting-women. In those days I could never have imagined missing her strict discipline and rigid code of behavior, but I missed her now. She'd been my mother's companion and my chaperon. She was something from home. Surely, if I asked Ennis to bring her to me as my companion and lady-in-waiting, he'd find a way. Or perhaps a better way would be to ask Garren Odonnel for her publicly as bride-gift. Permission wouldn't cost him anything.

The idea was cheering. All Starker IV knew Lady Agnes's strict propriety and rigid ethics. Lady Agnes would be able to come and go as she wished. Lady Agnes could carry messages, because everyone knew her ethics wouldn't permit her to betray her host or my husband.

Such thoughts kept me occupied, even after Ennis got up, and carried me as far as the Great Hall. Ennis and I separated at the door, for at this party we were host and hostess and there were too many guests for us to greet them all as a couple. The room was crowded, of course, though not, perhaps, as crowded as for the wedding. I took a deep breath and moved into the room, nodding politely to casual greetings, pausing to speak to members of the Houses who seemed to want more than a simple greeting, asking courteous questions of the Freemen I passed, acting the gracious Family hostess, as my mother had taught me to. I knew so few in this crowd and those I did know were enemies of my House. This made courtesy very difficult. No one from House deVree had come, of course. House Halarek had not come, either—everyone had heard Halarek was in mourning—nor had von Schuss. I didn't even see the electric blue of House Druma, though Druma was Odonnel's vassal as well as Karne's. But then, the Dukes of Druma had not been noted for their political courage for many generations.

I gave the Marquis of Gormsby a chilly nod, he who was party to my mother's death, and turned pointedly away when he opened his mouth to begin a conversation. The nerve of the man! It had been through his partisanship that Richard had been allowed to enter the Council chamber unsearched. How could the marquis expect me to conduct a civil conversation with an accomplice to Mother's murder?

In my fury at the marquis, I didn't watch where I was going and bumped into a Freeman wearing yellow and pale brown.

"Excuse me, sir—"

The man spun and shot out a hand to steady me. His dark eyes looked concerned. It was the short, stocky man from Lews I'd seen at the banquet. "Did the marquis presume on his relationship to Odonnel?" the man asked, then added, "I'm Klarence Duval, of Lews, as you can see. We have mutual friends." He waved a negligent hand toward two men standing beside one of the gallery pillars.

The two men made small bows and the one with the beard took a step toward Duval, a movement Duval stopped with a chop of his hand. "He's young and impetuous," Duval explained, nodding toward the bearded man. "He too seldom thinks of the dangers in a young and attractive Freeman approaching a noble lady, who everyone knows was forcibly married."

There was more to what Duval was saying than his words, but I couldn't figure out what. He was trying to deliver a double message, innocent on the surface, important underneath.

"The other gentleman has eye trouble," Duval continued. "He won't be able to stay here under these bright lights long." He turned briefly toward the men at the pillar and the Freeman from York ran one hand through his hair, then bowed again.

I stifled a gasp, recognizing the gesture as well as the man's shape. *Karne! Guardians protect him!*

Duval nodded his approval. I marveled at the man's ingenuity. "Eye trouble" had to mean the colored lenses Karne could only wear for a few hours. He couldn't have escaped notice here for even a moment without colored lenses. And the other merchant from Lews was Nik? It had seemed so last night, but last night was lost in the drug-fog.

The Freeman touched my hand in impersonal courtesy. "We hadn't thought to be able to approach you this day, but the press here isn't as great as we'd expected. If you'd come with me for a moment, our cities have small tokens of our best wishes in your marriage." His fingers closed briefly on my wrist in warning.

I nodded. I'd have to watch my reactions very carefully if the two men by the pillar were to leave Odonnel in safety. I took deep, steadying breaths as I walked. Karne and Nik! To see them now, after all these months alone among enemies.

The man in York colors took my hand and kissed it formally, then looked into my eyes. It *was* Karne! It was all I could do to keep my joy and fear inside me. Such a risk he'd taken!

Karne pulled a small wrapped gift from the pouch on his belt. "With the deepest wishes of my city for your happiness," he said.

I unwrapped the gift with trembling fingers. It was a rectangular packet of extremely thin paper and a delicate pen. The packet was small enough to be hidden almost anywhere. The paper was thin enough almost to disappear and soft enough it did not crackle. Secret note paper, if I found anyone I could trust with anything as incriminating as a note.

"My thanks, sir." I coughed delicately, putting my hand to my mouth and then to my throat. The slender packet disappeared into my bodice. "I have hopes that my lord husband will permit Lady Agnes to attend me now that I'm so near my time and safely married. Now I have paper to write her on."

"No need. That paper has better uses." Karne kissed my hand again and backed away. "Besides, the lady has been asked about the possibility."

Nik came forward then, bowed over my hand, and kissed it. "I regret that the gift I brought now seems inappropriate, my lady, but it's all I have," he said.

Nik brought his left hand up to meet his right, which was still holding mine from the kiss, and pressed a small, cold metal object into my palm. His hands fell away and I felt bereft.

"It would be best to look at my gift only after you're in your room, my lady," he whispered. His voice caught.

I resisted the temptation to rub his kiss against my cheek as a child would, and slipped my hand and its gift into my pocket instead. So close and yet so impossibly, permanently, out of reach. My fingers explored the gift. It was a small heart on a wrist chain, and I could not cry. To cry would draw unwanted attention to me and to the Freemen, and that could be fatal for them. I felt my face tighten with the effort of keeping back tears.

"I'll kill him!" Nik's whisper was not less frightening for its quietness.

I felt sick. Not Ennis. He couldn't mean Ennis, with his kind heart and dry humor and skillful hands! Ennis, who had saved me from Richard's plan. "No!" I whispered back. "He's my husband and the father of my child and I agreed to marry him in the ancient way. It was necessary. I love you no less."

The look in his eyes did not change.

"NO!" I said aloud and with all the emotional force I could manage.

He spun around and walked quickly away. Seconds later I felt a light touch on my arm. It was Frem Duval. He looked around to be sure no one was watching, then leaned toward me and spoke very quietly.

"My lady, I was too close not to hear." He glanced quickly around again. "Haakon"—he jerked his head toward Nik's vanishing back—"must have time to understand and adjust. He will accept your wishes. In time." He straightened so he was again at a polite social distance and spoke in a louder, social voice. "I imagine it's been lonely for you, with only men for company. Perhaps—'' He studied the floor for a moment. "Perhaps, my lady, a woman of your own age—" He hesitated again. "If your lord permits, perhaps you might now employ a lady-in-waiting, someone to take proper care of your hair and clothes. I doubt your old chaperon is any more skilled in such things than you.''

That embarrassed me because it was true. I should have thought of that myself. I must have shown either the embarrassment or the dismay, because Duval patted my arm in a paternal way.

"Nay, lady, I didn't mean to sound critical, but I know how women of the Nine are raised. I have a daughter about your age. If you mention her name, perhaps your lord would allow you her aid. She could be very useful, my lady.''

The look in his eyes and the intentness of his posture told me her usefulness would probably extend beyond hair and clothing. I looked toward Karne for reassurance. What did he know about this man? How did he get tangled up with a Freeman in the first place?

Karne smiled a very little bit. "I understand Adrian Duval is a skilled storyteller, my lady. She could ease the evening hours for you, especially after the child is born.''

So Karne approved. It would be good to have a woman to talk to. Lady Agnes was not a person one had conversations with: Her own opinions were too strong, too numerous, and too important to her. I let myself relax a little.

"If you'd write out her name and location, Frem Duval, I'll ask my lord husband if I may employ her.''

Karne looked relieved. Duval smiled approval.

"Very good, my lady.'' Duval scribbled a name and postal address on a scrap of paper from his belt pouch, handed it to me, and bowed in leave-taking. "We'll be leaving for home in the morning. We can't afford to take a week off for celebrating. A business runs best when the owner's present.'' He smiled again. "Well, good health, my lady, and may your child be born healthy as well.''

"Thank you, sir.''

"Don't give up hope,'' he added as he turned to go. "Don't ever give up hope.''

Karne turned and left with him without another word. That stung, even though I knew he could pay me no more than a stranger's impersonal attention. Yet the Freeman's last words gave me real hope. I hadn't been abandoned.

CHAPTER 8

Karne arrived at the pool first. He stood looking into the glassy water. He had thought it would help to see Kit. It had not. It had only made his dilemma, and hers, more frustrating. He could never get her out of House Odonnel. An afternoon of searching had found all exit stairs and lifts well-guarded. If she were moved to a less secure place . . . If she were moved to another holding, he would have a chance to get her back while she was above ground. Well, it could do no good to worry the problem here, when there was so clearly nothing he could do to get her out that would not result in both their deaths.

He raised his eyes to the edges of the pool. Reedy plants and imported trees from warmer worlds stood in pots along two sides, giving the effect of a jungle to the otherwise gray, stone-walled room. The pool had once been a giant aquarium for an Odonnel Lharr who had admired many species of large, bright-colored fishes from other worlds. Everyone had known about the aquarium because the Lharr had loved to show it off. In those days Odonnel children had swum and played with the fish. The Lharr himself had spent many hours over many years staring at the fish (and the children) through the glass walls of the pool. That Lharr had been long dead, but the pool had been maintained for its humidifying effects and for the children and the occasional Freeman or Gild guest who liked to swim.

Nik and Duval entered, laughing. Duval nodded politely toward Karne, dove directly into the water, and began splashing noisily toward the other end of the pool. Nik sat on the pool's edge with his feet in the water and motioned for Karne to do the same.

"Duval says that if there are bugs down here, and he doubts it, he'll make enough noise for whatever they pick up to be unintelligible."

Karne jerked his head toward the stout body thrashing toward the far end of the pool. "What's his interest in this? And why did you tell a stranger who you really are?" Karne could not keep the sharp edge from his voice.

Nik grimaced. "Last first. I wasn't raised to rule any more than you. Two cousins and an older brother were ahead of me, if you remember. But I didn't get your Academy training, either. Duval knew I was not from Lews and confronted me with it. The freecities always feel in danger from the Nine. Did you know that?" He didn't wait for an answer. "Like I said, I don't have your training and I couldn't come up with a false name fast enough to be convincing."

"You did come up with another name?"

Nik grinned sheepishly. "Uh-huh. But I made a mess of it, so I was really in trouble."

"You could've killed him."

"Now who's not thinking fast enough?" Nik's voice was angry. "This is a Freeman we're talking about, A *Freeman!* Not a man from an enemy House. Besides, it would've been a waste—he has valuable things to say—and it would've caused even more trouble than we're in now, because Freemen investigate such deaths."

Karne nodded reluctantly. "I'd forgotten that. No one investigates deaths among the Houses. Too much partisanship.

"What's Duval's interest in this?"

"His daughters. Once he heard what happened to Kit, he thought of his daughters and how he'd feel if something like this happened to one of them—though he knows they're supposedly safe because they're Freewomen—and said he would help us any way he can.''

"He's already done that.'' Karne thought of Duval's out-of-the-air offer of his daughter as maid and messenger.

Nik nodded. "It's more than softheartedness. He's begun to ask himself how much longer Freewomen can stay safe if the shortage of noble women continues. He thinks there'll be Sheet and Broken Seal marriages between the Houses and Freewomen within the next ten years.''

Suspicion stirred in Karne. The Freemen had been immune from the internal problems of the Houses for hundreds of years. "You believed that story? The danger is so minute—''

"Don't leap to such a conclusion, Karne. Intermarriage was common once. And I can believe he wants to protect his daughters. Freemen do love their children, usually, whether male or female. You yourself told me how much Odin Olafsson loved Egil and his brothers and sister. And my sire loved his children. Besides, Duval's an astute man and he has ideas about how we can rescue Kit.''

"Do his plans include his daughter?''

"Looks like it to me. As long as she carries nothing in or out, she should be safe enough. Perhaps he also wants to give her a look at what life as a lady of one of the Houses is like. From what I know of Freemen and their habits, the young woman won't find the life appealing.''

Nik kicked his feet slowly. Water swirled and rings spread outward. He watched Duval splash from one end of the pool to the other and back for some time before he spoke again. "He's concerned about more than his daughters. He's worried about the Old Party and their power in Council: They allowed murder in the Council chamber. Yet the Freemen are reluctant to interfere in what they see as the business of the Houses. Duval fears they'll hesitate until the Old Party is so strong that Freemen will be no longer free.''

Nik watched Duval some more, sharp lines appearing between his eyes. He sighed and turned toward Karne again. "The uproar at the Council where Richard killed your mother bothered Duval deeply, but other than voting that the Nine should never again hold the chairmanship, he didn't know what he could do. He's kept his eyes open since then for opportunities for the freecities to protect themselves better from the Old Party, though. He thought putting Richard in Breven would stop or at least slow the Old Party men down. It hasn't. Eventually he began to suspect that Richard isn't as isolated as he was sentenced to be.''

Nik's eyes followed Duval for several more lengths of the pool. "This past fall was time for Duval's biannual retreat. This year he went to the Retreat House at Breven."

Karne drew in a sharp breath.

"Aye. Not exactly, or not completely, for religious reasons." Nik faced Karne directly. "Richard lives in luxury there, Karne. He has whatever visitors he wants, apparently. Including women."

"Women? In Breven?" Karne tried to imagine even one woman in that all-male place. "There are six Retreat Houses for women. What can the abbot be thinking of!"

Nik's mouth twisted. "Money? Rich gifts? Maybe ingratiating himself with the temporarily deposed leader of the most powerful House on Starker IV? Those women don't come to Richard's cell to talk. They're common streetwalkers, from Loch, usually."

Karne's muscles bunched and he pressed his hands against the tiles to shove himself to his feet. Nik's hand shot out and clamped down on Karne's wrist painfully hard.

"Listen to this, Karne. The young deacon who was supposed to be guarding Richard's door told Duval a great lady had been expected to come and live in Lord Richard's cell for a time. Rooms were prepared for her in a secret place. She was expected at the end of Drak or the first part of Narn. Then Lord Richard told the young deacon that plans had changed. Nothing more than that."

"The first part of Narn," Karne whispered. "A great lady. Drak. The first part of Narn. Kit." Karne twisted out of Nik's grasp and sprang to his feet, so full of rage he did not know what to do. "Kit! He did originally intend to have her, just as Mother thought, but only to humiliate her and our House, not to marry her!" Karne let himself feel the fury for several minutes, then he suppressed it. "No man would've had her to wife after Richard had used her, so she would give Halarek no heirs. And the humiliation—Guardians! We'd never live down the humiliation!'' Karne stopped pacing and looked down at his friend. ''How can you tell me this so calmly? I'd've thought—''

''I'm calm *now*. I fought the sword-dummy in Odonnel's arena for most of the night last night, from right after Duval told me what had been planned to almost 'dawn.' ''

Karne grimaced, thinking of burning muscles and aching lungs. ''That ought to be enough to quiet you for a while. What you've told me is enough for me to owe Duval a large debt. Was there anything more?''

''Only that representatives from Kingsland and Gormsby visited Lord Richard during Duval's stay at Breven. And, of course, the vassals who are supposedly in charge of House Harlan now visited almost daily, one or another of them.''

''Damn them all to Hell and to Hel and Ragnarok, too!''

Nik snorted. ''That'll be too late to stop Richard. You may long be dead before Richard goes to Hell. That's his intention, that you precede him there.''

Karne ran a hand roughly through his hair several times. He stared down at Nik, his hair on end, his face grim. ''How did Ennis get Kit, then? What does he have that could turn Richard aside from a plan he's had for years?''

Nik stood. ''Only the Guardians know. Whatever it is, he has to be walking the sharp edge of a razor. He makes one mistake and he's doomed.''

''Not as long as she carries a half-Halarek child.'' Karne's voice was as hard as iron. Suddenly he could no longer stand the greenery and the tropical warmth of the pool. ''Let's get Duval and get out of here. I could use some work with the sword-dummy myself.''

''You can only use epees, remember,'' Nik said. ''Regular swords are not Freemen's sport.''

Fencing to exhaustion took the edge off Karne's rage, but only the edge. It was impossible to avoid imagining the humiliation and accompanying political losses if Richard had stuck to his original plan, and the imagining led to thoughts of what would have followed: Loss of Halarek prestige would lead to loss of vassals and markets, and that meant loss of power and cash, and that meant, finally, the end of House

Halarek. A weakened and humiliated House did not survive long. Six thousand people, more or less, would go into vassalage when Halarek fell, or serfdom if Halarek fell to an Old Party House. All Karne's personal family would be killed, because there could be no heirs of the old line left alive, nor any woman who could produce heirs. In the end, losing the fight with Richard would mean death for Karne and everyone he loved. The original goal of feud—inflicting pain and losses on the enemy—had changed since Richard. House Harlan now intended to *destroy* House Halarek, and Karne was not sure even Kit's legal marriage into Harlan would change that prospect much. Her child would be raised in Harlan, learning Harlan ethics and Harlan politics.

Nik and Karne left Odonnel before daymeal. Duval's information kept Karne's mind turning. All the way back to Gildport, Karne struggled to find a way to recoup this loss, to think of a way to free Kit. He could come up with nothing. Secured within House Odonnel, Kit was beyond possibility of rescue. *Almost* beyond possibility of rescue. Karne himself could see no way to infiltrate the manor, but perhaps Lady Agnes or Duval's daughter could find a weak spot in security arrangements. If Ennis Harlan allowed Kit to have ladies to serve her. If.

He shook his head. The ladies could provide information, but not escape. There was no effective attack on a Holding except by siege, and the recent wars on Harlan had put the expense of siege beyond Karne's reach. Only if Ennis brought Kit into the open, to Council, for instance, or to his family's smallholding, was there a chance to get Kit back, and that was a poor one more likely to kill Kit than to save her. Everyone knew the risks of traveling overland. Ennis would fly her if they moved, and knocking fliers out of the air was always very risky for the fliers' occupants.

Karne let Nik take the controls from Gildport to Ontar, his mind too preoccupied to fly safely. At Ontar's landing pad, all the household officers stood waiting. All were wearing black, as was right so soon after the baby's death. Then Karne's mind registered the discrepancies. Though his arrival required no household officers, all were there and their faces were rigid with restrained emotion.

Karne stepped out onto the flitter's wing reluctantly. He did not want to face more bad news. But dealing with bad news was the Lharr's duty. Sometimes it seemed as if it were his sole duty. He dropped onto the pad surface. Tane Orkonan was at his side immediately.

"My lord, I have the worst of news. There was no way we could've told you before now without causing your death and von Schuss's."

Karne looked into the face he had known since boyhood and saw grief and pain there. Tane had betrayed the depth of whatever tragedy had struck by using Karne's title rather than his name.

Tane swallowed hard. "There is also no way to soften the news, lord. I tell worst first. The Larga killed herself the day after you left."

Karne grabbed at Tane's sleeve to steady himself. The pad walls seemed suddenly to close in on him. "Why?" he whispered. "Why?" He felt Nik's steadying arm come around his shoulders.

"She told her ladies many times she knew she was never going to bear Halarek a living child. She said she couldn't bear the scorn of her family and yours any longer." Tane looked down at his toes. "She also left a note saying she knew you had broken mourning to go to your sister's wedding. She went on and on about that, as if you should have taken her, too, or stayed home. Which she meant was not clear. It was a long note she left, my lord, and very bitter."

Karne shut his eyes and clenched his fists. He took deep, shuddering breaths, but that did not quiet the chaos within. He had neglected his wife when she most needed support. He had put Kit's needs before Lizanne's and Lizanne had known it. He had been out of touch in Odonnel, deliberately out of touch, too soon after the baby's death. Now Lizanne was dead, too.

As if from far away, he heard Tane's voice saying, "It's not your fault. And Larga Lizanne was feeling very, very low, Karne. Dr. Othneil says that happens often with women after giving birth, even women who give birth to healthy babies."

Karne was to hear those words frequently over the next week. Lizanne had not been herself; he had made the choice necessary for Halarek's survival; it was not his fault; it was not his fault.

Yet, though he believed Dr. Othneil's insistence that postpar-
tum women sometimes killed themselves in fits of sadness
unrelated to what was actually happening to and around them,
the guilt did not go away. He had ignored her, almost entirely,
after the baby's death. He had left her alone with her grief. He
had put his sister's needs before his wife's. He would have to
live with that knowledge the rest of his life.

Odonnel accepted by tri-d announcement the offer of Lady
Agnes's help, on behalf of his guest, Ennis Harlan. Karne sent
notice to Lady Agnes of her new appointment the moment
Odonnel signed off. Karne felt quite sure he would not have
to use his position as head-of-House to *order* her to go. He
knew she had never been able to resist either a new baby or
the opportunities for lecturing that a baby presented. He was
right. She accepted eagerly, and her nephew agreed to bring
her himself from his smallholding south of the equator to House
Odonnel. That would be safer for her than arriving there in a
Halarek flitter.

That settled, Karne tri-ded Ennis to ask permission for Adrian
Duval to come and maintain Kit's clothes and dress her hair.
He regretted he had not known Kit would defend her husband
before he requested permission for Lady Agnes's service from
Garren Odonnel. The necessity of contacting the Lharr Odonnel
had grated, because it obligated Karne Halarek to do him a
favor of similar size at some future time.

Ennis Harlan accepted Adrian Duval's service immediately.
Karne told himself that Ennis accepted so easily because Kit's
request permitted Ennis to feel more powerful than the Halarek,
who had to ask *him* for such a small thing as a servant for the
Lady Kathryn.

The next day, House Halarek received formal word from
Odonnel that Lady Agnes had arrived safely. Similar notice
came about Adrian Duval's arrival on 1 Verdain. Only five
days later an urgent message arrived from Lews, hand delivered
to Halarek's fast-breaking in the Great Hall by a messenger in
Duval's own livery. Karne ripped the letter open right then,
oblivious to the curious stares of cousins at nearby tables. It
said the Lady Kathryn had been delivered of a daughter on 37
Kerensten. The child *appeared* healthy, but only time would
tell if that would last. Karne thought with pain of his own tiny

daughter, who had also seemed healthy at birth.

He reread the message several times. He looked on the back of the paper to see if Duval had added any other information. Nothing. He had to assume that if anything had gone wrong for Kit, Duval's message would have told him. He crumpled the paper in his hand. *A girl child. An heir, but not one who can rule. A woman can't speak in Council, even if the cousins would accept a female head-of-House.* Karne cursed and crumpled the paper in his hand. He wanted to throw something. In that much, had Richard succeeded. He had a child of Halarek blood under his control, and the child's father, not her uncle, would have the giving of her in marriage.

That thought reminded Karne of his own marriage. Lizanne was dead and he had not given his wife the mourning that custom required. The traditional mourning period must be observed, as well as countering Richard's moves permitted, and then he must marry again. He must set Orkonan to finding another suitable woman. Mourning would extend into Drak. He could not go to the Thawtime Council, then. Even if he had not been in mourning, he could not have faced either the sympathy of friends and vassals for the loss of his wife and baby, or the sly rejoicing of hostile Houses over Kit's kidnapping and delivery of a baby to Harlan. Years more of the Academy's training in emotion control could not have helped him with such a combination. Since Richard was out of politics, at least officially, the Council would probably do little of importance anyway.

If not Council, what could he do? Karne shut himself into the library, thinking. There had been no public announcement that Ennis and Kit's baby had been born. The omission was ominous. It probably also meant some other plan was being hatched to use Kit against her own House. A girl child was not as good a tool, even for Harlan, as a boy child. If Kit were to be used in another way, perhaps she would be moved from Odonnel. If she were moved, there would be a chance to get her back.

Karne took stylus and pad from the drawer in the table and wrote a letter to Duval, detailing his suspicions. Adrian had already been useful. Perhaps she could give advance warning of any new plan. Karne had not heard anything from Duval other than the news about the baby. He was sure that if the Freeman had discovered evidence that would convince Council that Richard was acting in defiance of his sentence, he would have let Karne know, because he himself could not have presented that evidence at Council, not this one, anyway. Duval could not act in Council without first getting the approval of his city's board. There had not been time for that yet. If he could convince the board at all. Freemen were very stubbornly set against "interfering" in what they considered the affairs of the Houses.

Karne called in Captain Rad, commander of Halarek's Specials, and ordered the Specials to prepare plans for a strike against fliers at a moment's notice, plans that would bring the fliers down with the least likelihood of injury to their passengers. Karne knew how slight a chance of success they had, but the planning let him feel as if he were doing something to help Kit. Yet if such a strike killed her—

It did not bear thinking about. Karne turned to the next piece of business, which was only slightly less repugnant than the thought of having to drag Kit's body out of a flier destroyed by his own men. As head-of-House, his duty was to provide a male heir to fend off internal warfare on his death. He ordered Frem Weisman and Orkonan to begin searching out candidates for his next wife. Fertility and strong health would be the most important criteria this time. He had proved himself a strong military leader since the Council at which he had been made Lharr. He had taken holdings from Harlan. He did not yet carry as much weight in Council as his sire had, but families with better blood than House Arnette's would now be willing to give him a daughter. The thought of marrying again soon sickened him, but Halarek had to have another heir. Kit's child could not be considered as long as she was in Harlan hands.

The immediate work taken care of, Karne called for his first food of the day. He was surprised to find it was daymeal. He had worked faster than he thought. He had intended to relax over the meal and put problems aside, but Richard would not be put aside. Until someone was willing to bear witness that Richard's sentence was not being served as Council intended, nothing would be done to stop him. And who, Karne wondered bitterly, really cared to stop the most powerful lord on Starker

IV, except House Halarek, House von Schuss, and a few Freemen? Who else would look for evidence of criminal blindness on the part of the abbot? Who would even suspect that a Retreat House would yield so easily to Harlan power? Someone had to bring the violations to Council's attention without Richard being forewarned. It would not be Freemen who did it, though more Freemen than nobility made retreats.

The answer of who would go to Breven to witness the violations, when it came, was so obvious that Karne felt amazed that neither he nor Nik nor Orkonan had thought of it before. The Councilmen from Lews and York would make a reappearance, on a retreat. If there was evidence to be had, they would find it, and Halarek and von Schuss would present it to Council. Excited enough to forget his grief for a little while, Karne called a page to bring Lord Nicholas von Schuss to the library.

CHAPTER 9

Karne and Nik prepared for their "retreat" carefully. Karne sent a private messenger to House Arnette with the announcement of Lizanne's death, an announcement he had not made earlier for fear that Lord Francis might profit from it in Harlan. Now Kit's child was safely born, the news of Lizanne's death had no value. Karne instructed the messenger to get lost on the way, so he would arrive after Karne's tri-d announcement explaining his absence from Council.

Next necessity, if Richard truly was in control at Breven, was an airtight cover story. Without one, Karne, at least, would be in great danger from Richard's men. Nik and Karne decided only Karne should go as an alderman and that Nik should go as himself. Aside from the fact that Karne could not appear as himself, the class differences might be useful. As Nik had said, Freemen did not trust the Nine and among the Nine, no one they knew had friends or even social acquaintances among the Freemen.

Another reason for Nik to go as himself was that Breven was the nearest male Retreat House to Holding von Schuss, and therefore was the logical choice for a retreat for Nik. It was not the nearest for his alter ego, Alderman Yrt of Lews. If Karsch and Yrt had decided to go on retreat together, the Retreat House east of Neeran was a more central meeting place. If the two went to Breven together, it would attract attention.

Business with the Heir in von Schuss, however, was an excellent reason for Alderman Karsch to make a retreat so far from home. Everyone knew how obsessed with business Freemen were. It would be natural for an alderman to come a great distance to make a social contact with a House that would be an excellent market for York's raw wool and wool rugs. The looms of von Schuss were famous for their fine woolen cloth and drapery goods. It was also widely believed that Baron von Schuss would carpet his entire manor, could he find enough rugs of superior design and quality.

By the morning of 9 Verdain, they felt secure in their cover story. The final step in preparation for departure was an official tri-d cast to Council Chairman Gashen. A Council call on an open channel would make what Karne said freely available to whoever tuned in, and all the Houses had someone monitoring the Council channel precisely so they could tune in when something came through. Karne, dressed in deep mourning, kept the announcement as brief as possible, because his pain was still too raw to hide for long, and a Gharr lord must never show pain.

He felt a flicker of shame that everyone watching would see the bleakness of Ontar's tri-d room, but he had had neither the time nor the money since becoming Lharr to make it more like the comfortable rooms visible in other Houses, both major and minor. Karne composed his face and posture, then signaled a tech to begin broadcasting. "I announce with great sadness the death of my wife, Lizanne Arnette," he said. "My House will be in mourning for my daughter and my wife until Drak. I'm sure you understand the kind of mourning such losses require. I myself will go into seclusion for at least two weeks. I feel my attendance at Council would show disrespect to my dead and deny the depth of my grief. I'll therefore not be attending Council."

Karne bowed toward the image of the chairman, who appeared to be sitting behind a desk in a room opening out of the center of the projection wall. The chairman nodded acknowledgment and signed off. For a moment, voices excitedly discussing or sadly commenting on the deaths in Halarek could be heard, then Karne motioned to the techs, who cut the communication links with the drop of a switch.

Karne turned to Nik. "We'll see what reaction that announcement brings. I wonder what House Harlan will do, now it knows officially that Lizanne is dead."

Nik's face was grim. "We'll get a chance to see what one Harlan does. Richard Harlan."

Karne had arranged with Orkonan to have meals sent to his quarters (where Orkonan or Weisman or Gareth could accept them from the servant at the door) and for one of those three men to visit periodically to create the impression Karne was inside in deep mourning. No one would consider such seclusion unusual. No one would suspect he had left the manor.

They arrived at Breven in a Gild flitter, a subtle announcement that the Freeman had gifted the von Schuss Heir with a flight in return for the Heir's listening to him talk about his merchandise as much as he cared to. Providing transport was a common practice, especially toward the lords of minor Houses, who saved money on fuel whenever they could. Karne had decided that, should any Freemen with a knowledge of wool happen to be at Breven, he would claim he did not mix religion and business. That excuse would also help explain why he and the Heir in von Schuss had come in the same flier: Karsch did not want to talk about business after they arrived.

Karne inserted the brown lenses just before a serf came to garage their flitter. A deacon met them, searched them for weapons and took Nik's stunner, then escorted them across the courtyard, through wide double doors and up a broad flight of stairs to the abbot's office. The abbot's secretary, a wrinkled, dried-up deacon, told them to wait in the antechamber.

"At the moment, the abbot has business associates with him," the secretary said. "Since you didn't notify us in advance of your arrival . . ." He then bowed toward Nik. "Had we known you were coming, my lord, we would certainly have provided a proper welcome and had accommodations ready." The deacon bowed again and left the room.

The abbot seemed in no hurry to finish his business. Karne

strolled over to one of the narrow windows. It overlooked a gravel beach and the ice-blue water of Lake St. Paul. Sun glinted and danced on the water. At the other end of the lake, and therefore visible only in imagination, lay the freecity of Loch in a deep forest of bluepines. Loch was the home of Councilman Davin Reed, who had spoken out against Harlan in Council on several important occasions. Reed, like Duval, was not so sure the Freemen would be eternally safe from the depredations of the Families.

The door of the abbot's inner office creaked as it opened. The abbot, a portly man in a habit of a darker gray than a deacon's, came out, still in deep conversation with two noblemen. Karne stiffened. He recognized the Lord of the Mark at once. The Lord of the Mark was Garren Odonnel's closest friend and a vassal of Richard Harlan. His "business" with the abbot must be very important indeed to keep him from Council. It took Karne several seconds longer to recognize the second man as Dannel of Jura, technically one of his own vassals, captured from Harlan the previous year. He kept his head averted to avoid any chance of Jura recognizing him. Jura had sworn fealty to him. He had laid his hands between Karne's and accepted the kiss of peace. He was breaking that oath merely by being in the Mark's company.

". . . and you can report to his Family that my lord of Harlan is being well-treated here," the abbot was saying. "If there is anything else I can do to make his stay here more comfortable, assuming, of course, that the Family will provide the means, I'll gladly do it."

Jura bowed and left the room.

My own vassal, Karne thought. Technically. Clearly I'll have to do something about him, and probably the others when I get back.

The Lord of the Mark muttered something in a dark tone. The abbot, visible from the corner of Karne's eye, frowned and shrugged. The Lord of the Mark scowled, but gave a curt bow and left the room, obviously unsatisfied about something. Karne turned back to the room when he heard the outer door shut. The abbot was greeting Nik. He did not bow to Nik, since theoretically they were of equal rank.

The abbot turned to Karne. "Freeman . . . ?"

"Karsch."

"Of York, obviously. I'll run briefly over our rules for you. There aren't many. This is a religious house, meant for prayer and meditation. Therefore everyone who comes here must wear a deacon's robes, so no one is distracted from thoughts of God by signs of differences in rank or financial standing. All robes have hoods. Men who wish to spend their time here in silence wear their hoods over their heads. The penalty for speaking to a hooded man is expulsion from Breven." The abbot stared hard at Karne, as though he had had much experience with merchants attempting to speak to the hooded. Karne looked at him coldly.

The abbot pinkened. "Visitors may come once per week, and must remain in the visitors' area on the level below us. Those are really all the rules we have. Meals are served in the refectory five minutes after a single chime of the bell. Worship takes place four times each day in the chapel and is announced by three chimes of the bell. On the occasion of a very important tri-d cast, all members of the community—and you're a member as long as you stay here—will be summoned by a runner. Do you have questions?"

When the two men shook their heads, the abbot clapped his hands twice and a young deacon entered the room quickly. "Deacon Benjmin, give these men robes and show them to their quarters."

The young man bowed and led the way out the door. Something about him niggled at Karne, but he could not clarify what it was that bothered him.

Karne and Nik were assigned rooms on separate floors. The young deacon gave Karne the key to a room on the third level and turned to take Nik somewhere else, muttering about short notice making it impossible to put the two men near each other. But when Nik insisted Karne come along to see where he would be, the young deacon insisted that Karne stay in his own room while the deacon escorted Nik to his. Nik gave up his protest and Karne obediently opened the door to his room and went in. It was a plain room, small and gray, with a plain but sturdy bed, a desk, and a single chair. The Sanitary was down the hall.

Karne waited many minutes for Nik to come back. When

he did not, Karne stepped out into the hall to see what he could see. All the men who came out of or went into nearby rooms were either Freemen or men from minor Houses. In the perhaps half an hour he waited for Nik, Karne saw enough coming and going to feel sure that no member of the Nine stayed on this floor.

Nik came briskly down the hall toward Karne, pulled him back into the room, and shut the door behind them. "The abbot has segregated the Nine from everyone else. There's no one but the Nine and the abbot on Level 2. We passed Richard's quarters, which had a Council guard outside the door, and Deacon Benjmin offered to introduce me later. He told me in a whisper that Duke Richard was not really inside at the moment, but was visiting friends on another floor. As if I'd approve." Nik's face and voice were stiff with outrage. "The young fool didn't seem to realize how that arrangement flouts Council sentence!" Then Nik looked around Karne's room and his face grew even angrier. "The abbot only mouths support for The Way's rules about no class distinctions, I see. Come. The room assigned me is very different. No wonder the deacon didn't want you to come along."

When Karne stood in the middle of Nik's assigned room looking at the thick rug, the soft upholstered couch and chair, he, too, felt very angry. Such favoritism was against all the rules of The Way. All men were equal in the eyes of God and were to be so treated. This was a re-creation of all of the comforts of the Nine. The room even had a fire burning in a fireplace. In a place as ancient as a Retreat House, it was probably a real fire. He was in no mood to test it.

"So much for the rules," Karne said, his voice low and vibrating with anger.

"And we haven't seen how Richard lives yet." The birthmark that was visible only when Nik was very angry or very hot stood out dark red from the top of his forehead back into his hair. He clenched his hand in the hair at the back of his neck, exposing the tail of the birthmark running down to the base of his neck. He shook his head. "I wonder where the abbot is hiding the wealth that must come from this perversion of the rules of The Way." His tone of voice reflected disbelief that a leader of The Way could behave so, and publicly. "What we've seen so far confirms what Duval told us."

Karne nodded. "He wouldn't have seen the Nine's rooms, either. Duval seems to have proven himself trustworthy. The Four Guardians know I need an ally among the Freemen!"

They had no more time to discuss the abbot's rule violations, because the bell for the evening meal sounded. The two men found the refectory by following the others on Nik's floor, perhaps a dozen, who wound slowly down two flights of stairs to ground level and a room toward the back, or lake side, of the Retreat House. Even here, nobles of the Nine sat apart, though they did not appear to get different food. With a silent nod of agreement, Nik and Karne separated to sit where assigned. Karne wondered why the men from the minor Houses did not protest the discrimination. He wondered, too, if Richard would eat with everyone else. If the abbot allowed the prisoner, who was supposed to be in solitary confinement, to visit other rooms, what would keep him from allowing Richard the company of his peers at meals? Duval had said Richard's imprisonment was lax.

Richard Harlan did not come to the refectory. His special treatment was not, then, general knowledge.

After the meal, Karne and Nik explored the Retreat House floor by floor. The chapel, refectory, visitors' area, game room, library, and various administrative offices occupied the ground level. Quarters for the Nine and the abbot's office (and his quarters? Karne wondered) took up the second level, where there were only ten doors still operable; the rest had been mortared shut. The minor Houses and the Freemen, of course, had the third level. The fourth level had open areas and rooms with large windows and would be truly useable only in high summer. In all Breven, there was no sign of Richard Harlan's presence other than the Council guard outside the rooms on Level 2. That was a cause for anger, too, that a Council guard had apparently been corrupted to serve the Harlan's whims.

Karne and Nik stood at last at a window on the fourth level, tired, disillusioned, watching the sunlight leave the greening slopes beyond Breven's wall. Each was lost in his own thoughts. A bell chimed three times. Vespers. The two men looked at each other.

"For appearances, because it's our first day?" Nik asked.

Karne nodded. "Probably a good idea, at least for me. Free-men are considerably more pious than most of the Houses are." Karne turned from the spring evening and headed without hurry toward the nearest stairs. "Meet me in this stairwell, after."

Nik went his own way down. It would not do an Heir of the Nine to be seen spending much time with a merchant.

Karne made his way to the chapel, where he stood at the back among the other Freemen. Nik, arriving later, walked forward to a place saved for the late among the Nine. They both slipped away the moment the pastor began the benediction. They stopped in the shadows of the stair's first landing.

"I've been thinking," Nik said. After a moment he added, with surprise in his voice, "A church service is a surprisingly good place for thinking." He paused again. "Perhaps we're looking for the wrong thing." He kept his voice low enough that the echo in the stairwell would not betray what he said. "Perhaps Richard doesn't even live in those rooms on Level 2 unless someone in authority at Council comes to visit."

Karne drew small circles on the landing with his toe. The sole of his boot made scratching sounds against the stone. "The abbot wouldn't dare violate Council orders that much." He looked up.

Nik met his eyes. "Wouldn't he? Richard could make the risk politically and financially worth it. And the abbot isn't stupid, really. We stumbled on his double standards only because of the game we play here. I'd wager no one knows there's a difference between the quarters for the Nine and for everyone else but the abbot and us. Do *you* know anyone of the Nine with even one friend among the Freemen? Or with any acquaintance with Freemen and their ways that goes beyond business?"

Karne shook his head. "So you're suggesting Richard's kept somewhere away from the general population so his conditions of captivity aren't noticeable?"

Nik nodded. "A deacon probably takes food and necessities in and out of that second floor room as if Richard really was there, just like someone's doing for you at Ontar. Perhaps the price of the deacon's silence about the arrangement is the extra food. The abbot certainly isn't generous with food if nightmeal was any indication." Nik jerked his head in the direction of the stairs going down. "We've looked for Richard everywhere else, shall we check below?"

They descended the stairs as fast as quietness allowed. On the next floor, a corridor stretched in both directions, broken only irregularly by doorways without trim or decoration of any sort.

"Split up?" Nik's voice did not sound at all sure that was a good idea.

Karne looked at the low lighting, the stark emptiness, the isolation. If Richard was living as far in violation of Council sentence as Duval believed, anyone who discovered that violation might be in considerable danger. He shook his head. "I wouldn't want to stumble on Harlan soldiers alone down here. Even as Freemen Karsch."

Nik moved left down the corridor. His hand fell to his stunner holster, then dropped to his side. The deacon had, of course, confiscated his weapon when he left his flier.

The two men reached the first turning in the hall without seeing so much as light coming from under a door. "All storerooms, probably," Karne said as they stood at the corner and looked down another stretch of hall just like the one behind them. "It would take a lot of food and linens and dishes to run a place this big."

Nik shrugged. "I wouldn't know. Uncle Emil and his seneschal take care of that sort of thing at home."

At the third turning they found a stairway going down. They stood in the stairwell doorway, listening. There was no noise at all from below. They looked at each other, then went down.

The stair came out at the end of a long dark hallway. Far down the hall, at the end, a pale light came around a corner, and with it, noise. Karne and Nik walked toward the noise. To their surprise, the hall did not turn at what had looked like a corner. It went to the left and straight ahead into blackness, but a wooden bar closed off easy passage straight ahead. The noise came from a lighted doorway about halfway down the left-hand corridor. Two men, robed as deacons, stood rigidly beside the door.

"They're dressed as deacons," Nik whispered, "but I'd bet you a hundred Gildcredits they're military. Look how they're standing. No civilian would stand that straight or that still."

Karne's heart lurched. Soldiers in disguise had to be Harlan soldiers. Harlan soldiers meant Nik could not investigate what was going on. No responsible soldier would let the friend of his master's worst enemy by him: *The friend of my enemy is my enemy.* If they were to prove Richard lived outside his sentence, if they were to prove the lights and party noises were Richard's, then he, Karne, would have to go down there alone. Karne's heart pounded harder. His palms felt clammy. Richard had sharp eyes and a sharper mind. Would brown lenses be enough to fool him?

Karne wiped his palms against his hosen. Richard must be stopped. He might recognize Karne, but that was a chance Karne would have to take. He was looking at possible discovery, possible death, versus certain death for him and his House if Richard's plotting were not stopped. He wiped his palms dry again and started down the hall toward the light.

Nik's hand clamped down on his arm, stopping him. "Where the devil do you think you're going!" he snarled, the sounds all the fiercer for being quiet.

"I have no chance of producing an heir for a year or more. Kit has produced one and could produce another in that time and she's under Harlan control. It's vital to Halarek to know if control means *Richard's* control. Duval says it does. If he's right, someone has to stop this by reporting what's going on to Council."

"So the Lharr Halarek is going to go into a nest of Richard's toadies and friends? You're out of your mind!"

Karne twisted free. "I'm Alderman Karsch of York. I'll be able to pass as that, as least for a short time. *You'd* be recognized at the door. You'd never get in. If that's all that happened to you. You're your House's only heir, too."

"Karne—" Nik took a hard step forward.

Karne gave him a hard look. "The presence of the Heir in von Schuss can't fail to raise a stir, no matter who Richard has with him. The risk is less for me. No one among the Nine looks at Freemen very closely." Karne looked away, uncomfortable. "Besides, I need you to stay clear, to be able to report to Council if I'm discovered. If I've misjudged my disguise, or what's going on down there . . ."

Nik made one last try. "You think Richard won't recognize you?"

"I don't intend to get close enough to Richard for him even to notice me."

Just then, a woman's shrill screech made them jump. Both of them pressed flat against the wall in case the guards should look their way. Raucous laughter followed the screech. Karne motioned for Nik to stay where he was and moved ten meters closer to the light. The guards had been shaken out of their guardpost rigidity. Several minutes passed, then a buxom woman in a diaphanous green robe came to the guards, still laughing, and handed them a large bottle. She retreated back toward the light.

"Guardians—!" Nik choked off whatever he had thought to say afterward. "A woman," he continued in a whisper. "In Breven! Duval's more right than I wanted to know!"

"By my Mother's Blood! Duval was right. Council will be more likely to believe one of the Nine than a Freeman though." Karne knew that member of the Nine had to be him. He summoned his courage and walked down the hall, trying to look casual and confident. He had never before had to walk into such danger unarmed. Never.

When he had come even with the guards, he opened his deacon's robe to expose York's colors. The guards patted him for weapons and let him pass. Karne filed away in his mind that apparently not everyone was searched for weapons in the courtyard.

Ahead of him, two young men in deacon's habits lounged on the floor against the sides of an open doorway. They were drinking something from a leather pouch and laughing loudly. One of them was Deacon Benjmin. The woman came out again. She bent from the waist and offered the young men food from a tray, exposing the most delectable of her charms at the same time. When she straightened, she saw Karne and gave him a bold smile. The five-pointed star of the professional courtesan glittered just below the woman's breastbone, the gold star that indicated highest quality.

Karne did not respond to the smile. He could not. According to Duval, this was the fate Richard had planned for Kit, time in his rooms as if she were a common harlot, then return to her family. Perhaps he would have gone so far as to mark her with the star. It was hard to believe he would even consider that, yet he had already gone far beyond anyone's expectations.

Karne felt a little sick. If Duval had not warned Nik about Richard, what would have happened? Kit had had a baby girl. What did Richard plan now for Halarek and for Kit? Well, he couldn't find out anything standing outside the door. He must see Harlan, and others of the Nine he was sure, eating and drinking and laughing, entirely in violation of Council sentence. He must witness to Council what was really happening at Breven.

CHAPTER 10

I lay quietly in bed and listened to the careful movements of Lady Agnes outside the bedcurtains. She was trying to be quiet but the hard soles of her shoes made slapping sounds against the stone floor as she moved around the room. She had arrived a week before little Narra was born and had been a blessing since. I'd never thought to see Lady Agnes as a blessing. I'd always been too much of a tomboy for her taste, but her rigid propriety made her an ideal choice in Odonnel's eyes. All of Starker IV knows Lady Agnes and the strictness of her ethics and sense of propriety. She's the careful parent's model chaperon. No one but the Halareks would suspect she'd give me the slightest help in escaping my prison. It *was* a prison. Ennis was a good husband and father and no one treated me badly, but I could not leave my suite of rooms, even to go across the hall to Ennis.

Even if I could have, there was no chance of escape from House Odonnel. There's no chance of escape from any House without insider help. None at all. Even the War more than a hundred years ago hadn't breached any of the Houses. How could my brother and any army, then, hope to break in where the big bombs could not?

I heard Lady Agnes settle into the chair beside the bed. The chair creaked, and then I heard the soft little hum she used when rocking the baby. The delivery had been hard, though Lady Agnes assured me that was normal for a first child, and I was still very tired from it.

I went back to sleep. I'd been sleeping a lot, and alone, since the baby was born. Ennis slept across the hall because, he said, my body needed to rest and heal before we resumed coupling. When I opened my eyes again, it was to Lady Agnes's gentle shaking. She held out Narra to me and I took her under my blankets so she could nurse in warmth. Lady Agnes opened the bed curtains and asked the guard outside to have daymeal sent up. After Narra fell asleep, Lady Agnes took her from me, burped her, and laid her in the elaborately carved cradle Ennis had made. The beautiful cradle was one proof that he'd spoken truly when he said he wanted children.

Lady Agnes came back to the bed, shook out the dressing gown that lay over the arm of her chair, and held it for me to slip into so I wouldn't be cold while I used the Sanitary. Her kindness brought tears to my eyes. Tears came far too easily these days. Lady Agnes said that, too, was normal after a birth, but in all the years I'd known her, she had seldom been kind, and I felt uncomfortable when she was. Life is often hard for women of the Nine, and Lady Agnes makes sure her charges are well prepared. Kindness, especially from Lady Agnes, rarely lasted long.

"You have a guest arriving soon, Kathryn." Lady Agnes's voice was calm and lacked its usual bite. "The waiting-woman Lord Karne arranged to send you will arrive in less than an hour."

The news stunned me for a moment. Two large concessions from Odonnel in less than two weeks' time—Lady Agnes and now a waiting-woman—were more than I would ever have expected. The concessions hadn't even needed Ennis's intervention! The fact that I had female companions was, at the moment, more important than Odonnel's reasons for granting them. I was going to have a guest at least! She would be my waiting-woman if I liked her. Perhaps she would become a friend, too, as one's former nurse/ governess/ chaperon can never be.

I braided my hair, then splashed cold water on my face to make me feel more alert. I was getting better at braiding, but it was still not the tidy braid Tamara or Donna would have made. Lady Agnes was worse at braiding than I: She had had about thirty more years than I of having a waiting-woman do her hair. I tossed the braid over my shoulder, selected a thick slice of crusty, buttered bread and a round orange fruit from the daymeal tray beside the door, and sat on the bed to eat.

"You'll get crumbs in your sheets," Lady Agnes remarked, looking up from her knitting. This was more like the Lady Agnes I had grown up with.

While I ate, I let myself imagine what the waiting-woman would be like. Taller than I, graying, a gentlewoman skilled with clothes and hair and needing work due to some family tragedy or to her husband's wasteful habits. Karne knew how important my appearance was to me. What I looked like at the wedding had probably been quite a shock to him. Ennis had done his best to help, but his help, except as a mirror, was no help at all. (If noblewomen know little of such things, how much less does a noble*man* know?) Ennis's House and House Odonnel, too, had been most stingy with wardrobe and hair-dressing help; they had provided nothing but that horrid wedding dress.

Feet shuffled outside the door and voices spoke quietly. The door opened and the guard outside waved a young woman into the room. Odonnel's seneschal followed her. He bowed, but before he could say anything, the young woman had made a brief curtsey.

"Peace be on this house, lady," she said.

"And on yours," I answered.

"May I present Adrian Duval of Lews," the seneschal said.

The young woman curtseyed again, slowly and gracefully. Then she stood up, patted a hair from the dark knot at her nape back into place, and smiled a long, lazy smile. "I'm delighted to meet you, Lady Kathryn. Your brother has told me a lot about you." Her voice was husky and languid. "I tell a good tale, either real or imagined, and I know how to dress hair and body in becoming fashion. Lord Karne said you could use both.''

I felt Lady Agnes bristle. Frew Duval's remark wasn't a slight, not really. Lady Agnes's ideas of style, even her idea of proper subjects for a lady's conversation, were a generation out of date. Karne had just been stating the truth about the way I looked. Adrian Duval's fashion sense showed in her clothes. Her cherry-red gown, though it complied with the Houses' regulations concerning modest dress and revealed no skin at ankle or wrist or neck, fit her perfectly and flattered her complexion. The necklace and earrings she had chosen suited the dress and the circumstances, which were, essentially, a job interview in a noble House. The small mirror that dangled from a ribbon at her waist suggested a new fashion had appeared in the months I'd been shut away.

I liked her voice, her style, her languid manner. Her warmth would be a pleasant contrast to Lady Agnes's admonitions and injunctions. When Lady Agnes returned to her customary a-cerbic mode of behavior, that was. Better yet, Adrian was a Freewoman, and that meant she was not bound by Family alliances and enmities. I wouldn't have to watch my tongue every moment to protect my House from tales she might carry to hers. And the tale-telling of the other sort, if she were truly as good at it as she said, might make staying up past nightmeal worthwhile. Evenings had been boring. Lady Agnes knew no stories for people over the age of twelve, Odonnel allowed me neither letters nor tri-d, and books were scarce. Storytelling after nightmeal was a common practice in the Houses. I was surprised to learn Freemen indulged in it.

This arrangement would be extremely unusual, of course, a Freewoman working for a noble House. I couldn't remember ever meeting a Freewoman.

I turned to the hovering seneschal with as much charm as I could manage at the moment. ''Thank you. Tell your master Frew Duval will suit me very well.'' I waved him out of the room.

''My trunk,'' Adrian called after him. She turned back with a smile and handed me a note. ''I was optimistic about the job,'' she said, ''so I brought my things.'' The note said: ''My father and your brother have similar political goals. My father is the councilman from Lews. You met him briefly at your wedding. I can serve as go-between, or spy. That was my father's intent. Destroy this note.''

I looked at Adrian. Her eyes flicked quickly around the room. Her question was plain: Are there spy devices?

Were there? I didn't think so. That some of the servants spied I had no doubt. Some of ours did, too. I felt a smile break out. I'd finally be able to tell Karne what was happening.

The outside guards, grumbling, carried in a sturdy trunk and set it with a loud thump in the middle of the rug. Adrian pressed a coin into each man's hand as he left. She looked around the room until the door shut behind the men, then she slid traveling gloves from her hands and looked around the room. ''Where should I put my things?''

I pointed to the alcove she was to share with Lady Agnes, which was separated from the main room by a heavy tapestry. She unpacked her trunk into the dresser emptied for her use, then sat on the lid of the trunk and began to write a letter. She licked the seal, then called a guard to give it to a messenger. My heart stopped. Could anyone be so dumb as to expect to send a letter from my quarters anywhere outside Odonnel/ Harlan? Garren Odonnel wouldn't let word about the baby get out before he was ready to announce her birth himself. He could kill Adrian for treachery, for spying, for any crime he dared to dream up if she spoiled his carefully timed announcement, and by the time the aldermen of Lews found out about her death, it would be too late.

''I promised my father I'd write him the moment I was settled to tell him I arrived safely,'' she told the burly man who answered her call. Her manner was girlish and a little naive.

The guard looked at Adrian with something near maliciousness and demanded that she open the note and read it to him.

''Can't you read?'' she asked sweetly.

He slapped her. ''Women keep their places in *this* House,'' he snarled. ''Read it!''

Adrian looked at him in amazement for a moment, then threw such a right to his jaw that he staggered. He would have hit her again, but I stepped between them, and he didn't dare hit *me*.

In Halarek, that guard would have been executed (in my

sire's time) or expelled from the holding without references (Karne's way), which was perhaps worse. In Odonnel, had I not had Ennis's protection, we women would have paid for Adrian's retaliation and my intervention. Adrian didn't seem to know that, or at least she didn't act afraid. She slit the seal, cleared her throat, and began to read.

"Dear Father, I have arrived safely and have met Lady Kathryn. I performed as you bade me, especially a deep curtsey for the lady. The dress I arrived in is in excellent condition, it being, as you know, made of special material from a unique factory. I will write later about how I like it here. Your loving daughter, Adrian."

The soldier looked disappointed. I felt weak with relief. The letter had the tone of a coddled child. Adrian was watching the guard, and I thought I saw satisfaction flit across her face. She looked him in the eye. Her manner was now that of a confident and well-protected woman.

"I live here under Council protection, prefet, and Lharr Garren agreed I could write to my father whenever I wanted as long as I said nothing political and sent no information that could injure House Odonnel. You've seen the letter. My father will expect it within the next three days. That gives you time to show it to the Lharr Odonnel if you must."

The guard's mouth thinned. I would've been willing to bet he'd been planning to threaten her with showing the Lharr the letter. Now she'd beat him to it.

"Lord Ennis will check with Frem Duval in three days' time to see that the letter was sent," I added for good measure.

The guard snatched the letter from Adrian's hand and stalked out.

I looked at the dress that had been the main topic of the letter. It was top-grade narsilk, but only narsilk. There was no special material in it, not even in the trim. I tentatively ran a finger down her sleeve. No special weave either . . .

It was a code! She had a prearranged code about the dress! It would have been in terrible condition, in spite of its "special" fabric, if my baby had died. I thought the reference to my union with Ennis as a "unique factory" was pretty funny. How could I show my understanding and appreciation? I didn't need to. She closed the distance between us and gave me a big hug. I hugged back, then she stepped away and set about changing out of her traveling clothes.

Adrian settled immediately into my life in House Odonnel. She moved with lazy grace, but her slow and languid movements belied her sharp and devious mind—as the note home, designed to be boring to males, showed. She was charming to Ennis, loved the baby, learned to manage Lady Agnes's fits of lecturing with equanimity. In fact, if there's one word that succinctly describes Adrian Duval, it's "equanimity."

Adrian brought hope, as her father's parting words after my wedding had. My life in Odonnel was peaceful, and I liked and respected Ennis, but accepting the fact that my child would be raised by enemies was extremely difficult for me. With Adrian's letter-writing privilege and skill at hidden messages, I could and did tell Karne through Duval when important things happened. This alone was a great relief to me.

I should have known such calm could not last. Adrian had been with us about a month when Ennis awakened me intentionally when he came to bed in the early hours of the morning. He lay partway on me to keep me from moving and kept his hand over my mouth until I was awake enough to be quiet on my own.

"Listen, Kathryn," he whispered, "Garren says you're to be moved within a day or two. He didn't say where, but he did say he didn't think I'd want to go. He knows I love you, you see." He dropped his forehead onto my shoulder and I could feel him composing himself. He had never said the words before, though he had shown his love in hundreds of ways. "I have sources in this House and mine," he finally said, "and the word is, Richard isn't happy that you're not pregnant again. He intends to make you pregnant himself this time."

"He can't!" I whispered back. "I'm your wife! He wouldn't so disgrace his own House."

Ennis lifted himself onto his elbows so he could look down at me. "It's only a disgrace if other people know about it. That's Richard's philosophy. And if he's in Breven, a *men's* retreat, who would suspect he has a woman? Afterward, I can act as if the child he begets is mine, which would be tidier, or you can become a widow and therefore free for the taking. It makes no difference to Richard. His power is such that I can't defy him directly. Garren won't defy him, either, though this is too much for even his stomach.''

I felt as if all the blood had left my head. Richard himself. For a moment the already dark room disappeared entirely. I heard Ennis's voice as if he were far away.

''Why do you think you've been in Odonnel all this time? To keep you farther from Richard. Odonnel is my mother-House, once removed, but I've run out of people to ask favors of and debts to call in. After today, I can't keep you safe anymore.'' Ennis suddenly rolled onto his side and crushed me tight against him. His voice was fierce in my ear. ''I'd die for you if it would help, but it won't. I've just called in my last debt. Even that may not get you and Narra away safe. We're joining a caravan, but we must be gone before the sun rises in order to meet it and Narra must not cry or we're lost.''

Ennis hugged me hard. ''It was hard enough accepting Richard having the training of Narra. I can't accept what he plans for you.'' He squeezed until I felt my joints pop. ''Do you have any idea how much I love my two girls?'' he whispered in my ear.

He sprang from the bed, turned on the lights, and began assembling the minimum of necessary equipment. I forced myself to think. If Odonnel was planning to move me, he would do it in absolute secrecy, because any move onto the surface risked my recapture. Karne must be told about the move as soon as possible. Could either or both of the women take word out? Would they be allowed out after we escaped? How was Ennis going to manage our escape? How could we even pass the guards outside the door, especially with the baby, without being betrayed?

I awakened the other women and told them we were leaving. We decided among us that Lady Agnes and Adrian would both carry messages to Karne. Once Ennis and I were gone, the ladies would certainly be sent home. Wouldn't they? Neither had any value as a hostage, though Odonnel might hold them several days to keep them from informing Karne as long as possible.

Or he might hold them until we were caught.

CHAPTER 11

Karne hovered at the door of Richard's suite for several minutes, acting as if he were hesitant to thrust himself into the raucous company. After all, what would a Freeman know of parties among the Nine? Karne did need to assess the crowd before entering it. If he were to be the only Freeman inside, he would draw too much attention to himself, especially from the host. Richard's intelligence and sharp eyes would give him a very good chance of identifying his clan enemy. If that happened, Karne was dead, even here, in a Retreat House. The abbot would find some way to explain the murder as an accident or as self-defense. The man's future income depended on it. And he was, in addition, an Odonnel cousin.

Tapestries and heavy draperies of rich cloth decorated the walls of the suite. Elaborately carved wood tables supported piles of food and huge bowls of drink. A deacon with a concertina provided music, almost inaudible amid the chatter and laughter. Everywhere, people in various stages of intoxication talked, sang, petted, or danced—alone or in pairs. The smells of sweat and intoxicants hung in the air like smoke. There were four or five Freemen present. Karne felt a moment of anger at their knowing violation of Council sentence and inwardly cursed their stupidity in putting profit before the danger of supporting such a flagrant violation, but in the end, he was grateful. Their stupidity and greed would allow him to spy on Richard.

When he could see well enough, Karne dropped a handful of silver pennies into the extended hands of the deacons beside him and stepped into the room. Deacons, whether here by vocation or by parental compulsion, had little money to buy small pleasures, let alone large ones. Allowing the deacons at the door to take admission money put them in Richard's debt.

Karne looked first for Richard. He did not see him. He felt suddenly cold. Perhaps his assumptions had all been wrong and this was merely a gathering of aberrant deacons and their guests. Perhaps the favoritism in room assignments was just that. Perhaps Duval had been wrong. Perhaps Duval had deceived him for reasons of his own. Karne felt colder. Duval was sending his daughter to Kit. Could that be what he had been after, a connection to Kit for some reason? Or to House Odonnel? The possibilities were terrifying. Karne clenched his hands to steady himself. If Duval had sent a spy or assassin to Kit . . . Karne shut his eyes, swallowed hard, then opened his eyes again. Kit was clever and resourceful. There was nothing he could do to help her where she was.

The crowd swirled around tables of food and bowls of punch. A crowd also clustered in one corner of the room. At first Karne could not see what attracted so many people. He moved closer. When several guests drifted away from the group, Karne could see Richard Harlan sitting on an upholstered bench, one arm around the buxom woman who had come to the door, the other beckoning to a deacon for more drink.

Karne's first feeling was relief. Duval had been telling the truth. Kit was safe from any plotting on the Freeman's part. His relief did not last. The luxury of the suite, the crowd of people, the woman—all were against the rules of The Way as well as Richard's sentence. Karne felt hot and violent. Richard had been sentenced to nine years in a small bare room for solitary contemplation of murder and its consequences. The sentence had been perverted to meaninglessness. His mother had *died* at Richard's hand and Richard was still drinking and whoring and having fun with his friends.

This *was* a group of Richard's friends. Karne recognized one of Garren Odonnel's first cousins, a lord from House Kath, the Lord of the Mark, Ingold Kingsland, and the Heir in Gormsby, whatever his name was. Karne forced away the urge to smash and kill. He had a role to play here and he must stick to it if he wanted to live to see the dawn. There was much to learn here—how Richard managed to sneak a woman into Breven, for example—but he must act quickly. He was nearing the end of his time limit with the lenses.

He strolled over to a punch bowl. I am a wool merchant from York, he told himself, firming the role, fitting himself into it. I don't conduct business on retreat, but there's no harm in meeting potential customers. This is high company for me. I must be properly appreciative of the opportunity the abbot's given me.

Once settled by the punch table, however, Karne felt reluctant to move, in spite of his intentions to mingle with the guests. He had an excellent view of the crowd and the punch bowl, by its nature, encouraged brief and superficial conversations. In addition, there was probably less chance of being asked a technical question about wool if he stood in such an obviously social place.

He heard nothing of value while he stood there, only gossip, and Odonnel/ Harlan gossip at that. He did clearly identify men from the Houses of Langlek, Berden, Leat, Emmen, Rhiz, Kerex, Lynn, Skabish, and Brassik in the crowd. Harlan or Odonnel vassals, most of them. The last three were especially disturbing to see, because within the last two years they had become Karne's vassals by right of conquest.

So what's news about that? he asked himself bitterly. I learned very quickly after I came home that I can't turn my back on anyone. *Halarek's* vassals taught me that.

The lenses began to feel scratchy. Karne's eyes burned. Frustration tore at him. The longer drink flowed, the looser tongues would get, but he must leave to protect his eyes. Just then the crowd fawning on Richard shifted and murmured, then Richard and the woman disappeared into an adjoining room. They were out again within twenty minutes. The woman was flushed, breathing hard, and bundled into a deacon's robe and hood. The Lord of the Mark and the Gormsby Heir hurried her out the door.

Deacon's robes! That's how he does it!

Outrage mingled with a reluctant admiration for Richard's ingenuity. Then Karne remembered Richard's original plan for Kit. *This was how he had planned to get Kit in here! Put her in gray and keep the hood up. No one would speak to such a person or even look too closely. It would have worked! By all the Guardians, it would've worked!*

Karne trusted himself in the room no longer. The new knowledge was too much even for his Academy training. He excused himself abruptly from the men he had been speaking nothings to and left. He brushed past the deacons at the door with a brusk "good night" and hurried into the safe darkness of the hallway. Before he had time to calm down, Nik had grabbed his arm and tugged him further away.

"They took that deacon past the barricade," Nik whispered, his voice harsh and urgent. "The sign says 'Warning! Tunnels of the Old Ones. Booby-trapped. Danger! Stay out!' And they took that deacon down there."

"That wasn't a deacon." Karne took many deep, slow breaths. The temerity of Richard, bringing a woman into a Retreat House! The horror of knowing it could have been Kit . . .

"That was Richard's whore." Karne's voice shook in spite of him. "I'm sure that's how he intended to bring Kit in and where he intended to keep her until he figured his revenge was complete." Karne felt Nik stiffening and went on, partly to give his friend time to regain control. "Everything Duval told us seems to be true. Only Duval didn't know how bad things really are here."

Karne drew Nik toward the stairs, reciting what he had seen as they went. Nik stumbled after him, his body moving as if against great resistance.

"I'll kill him," Nik was muttering. "I'll kill him, kill him, KILL HIM!"

"Hush!" Karne snarled. "We're outnumbered and this *isn't* friendly territory."

In the stairwell, Nik dug in his heels. "I'm going back. I

want to see what sort of place that snake intended to keep Kit in while he—'' Nik slammed the soft side of his fist into the wall.

Karne listened to Nik's heavy, rapid breathing. When it had slowed and evened, he said quietly, ''I brought a light.'' Then he added, ''How will you know what path's safe? The tunnels of the Old Ones are deadly.''

''I know. I figure Richard's men are the only ones who've used that tunnel in years, maybe hundreds of years. They'll leave tracks in the dust.''

''God go with you.''

They clasped hands, hard, briefly, then Nik took the light and disappeared into the shadows back toward Richard's suite. Karne thought briefly of the strange rectangular device Egil had left with him, a device which Egil said disabled the traps in the Old Ones' tunnels. He would not tell Karne how he came by it, though. Richard was using such a tunnel. Egil had captured Richard after he escaped from Breven. Perhaps Egil had taken the device from Richard before he brought him back. On the other hand—

The Lord of the Mark and his companion reappeared as bulky shadows at the end of the hall and vanished around the corner toward Richard's suite. Karne felt relieved, because he was standing in the only stairwell, and deeply disturbed, because the two men were clearly staying the night and not as official guests of The Way.

Perhaps there are other women, he thought. Perhaps Richard's turned the lowest level of Breven into a brothel. He put a rein on such thoughts. That wouldn't be Richard's style at all. Richard's style was to flaunt privileges that were his alone. No, there would be no other women and the one woman would be first-class and strictly for Richard's personal use.

Nik was a long time returning. Karne reluctantly considered the possibility that something had happened to him, that Nik had encountered the Lord of the Mark coming out, perhaps, or run afoul of one of the Old Ones' traps. The Old Ones had loaded all the tunnels under their buildings, now ruins, with traps. All the traps had mechanisms for resetting, so they had not been intended as a one-time defense against some enemy, either. No one had ever found out what they *were* protecting.

Some men believed they were protecting great treasure and risked the dangers of the tunnels to look for it. That was how the Gharr knew so much about the variety of traps the Old Ones used, from the corpses.

There were floor traps—shallow holes filled with sharp staves, deep wells with water out of sight at the bottom, combinations of hole and falling slab. Some of the traps were sections of wall that closed off the tunnel into a tiny box that soon ran out of air. Others were boulders that crashed to the floor, pulverizing whatever was underneath. Karne had seen a Zinn bear under one of those once, a bear Karne and his brothers had been tracking. Karne also remembered the night of his return to Starker IV, when Richard's planes shot down his and Nik's flitter and all their escort fliers over Zinn. Karne had hidden in the outer end of an Old Ones' tunnel that night. He had been afraid of it, but he had preferred it to what Richard would have done to him and he had felt his way very carefully just out of sight. Richard had ordered one of his soldiers to follow Karne. The soldier had been so terrified of the Old Ones' traps that he fell down the stairs into the ruin, then refused to go farther, chancing what punishment Richard would give him rather than pursue Karne; and Richard's punishments were notorious for their cruelty and originality.

What's keeping Nik? Karne asked himself. He can't have fallen into a trap. They make a loud noise, or the victim does.

He finally could wait no longer to take out the lenses, grateful that the lens cases had "L" and "R" embossed on their lids so he could feel which was which. His eyes immediately felt better, but now he must keep his hood up, and with the hood up, no one would speak to him. Moments later voices moved toward him.

Karne muttered a curse and ducked into the blackness under the stairs. Isn't that the way it always happens? he thought savagely. The minute I take the lenses out, someone shows up who makes having them in necessary.

Four or five men, from the voices, came into the stairwell and went upstairs. The party was apparently breaking up. Almost on the heels of the first group, a second group of men came into the well and went up the stairs. Nik followed close behind.

"Karne?" he whispered into the darkness after the men were well gone. "Karne, are you here?"

Karne stepped out of the darkness. Nik jerked his head toward the stairs. "Let's go to my room and talk. You won't like what you'll hear."

Nik had no sooner shut his door behind them than he burst out, "Richard has the harlot half a kilometer down that tunnel and there are five sprung traps between the Retreat and the room. Richard sacrificed five men, at least—there may be more sprung traps beyond where I stopped—to find a safe path. Five men! So he could destroy Kit!"

"And Halarek," Karne added softly.

"Aye, that, too."

Nik leaned over the small table beside the door, his fingers gripping the edges. Karne saw his knuckles turn white.

"Karne, he has her *name* painted on the door. Kit's. 'The Lady Kathryn Magdalena Alysha Halarek.' And he keeps that whore in there!" The table creaked with the pressure Nik was putting on it.

Karne swallowed hard and prayed he would never love a woman so much that just the idea of injury to her would tear him up as love was tearing Nik. "He won't get her. She's safely married, Nik. Even Richard won't violate that. Not, at least, when she's married to a relative."

"I have to get out of here," Nik said, "or I'll kill him. The cost of that, to my House and your hopes, would be far too high. I can't even challenge him to a duel, because he's under Council sentence."

"You'd be outmatched, Nik."

"So I'd be outmatched. If I killed him, if I only managed to geld him—"

"Think!" Karne snapped. "So you'd have the satisfaction of hurting him before he killed you. What would happen to House von Schuss with its one remaining Heir dead? It would go into Council hands, and you know in whose hands the choice of a new baron would be. Think, Nik!"

"I'm going to have an emergency at home that prevents me from completing my retreat now," Nik mumbled. "I can't think here. I can't stay in the same building with that slime, knowing what he intended for Kit—'' His voice broke off in pain.

Karne could see no further point in staying, either. They had seen enough. With luck, he could convince Council to post Council guards on Richard or to increase his sentence or, much less likely, order him to serve out his sentence in the Desert of Zinn as any serf or slave would have to do. The thought of what that humiliation would do to the already wobbly alliance of vassals in House Harlan gave Karne momentary pleasure. He must plan each step toward convincing Council carefully, though, and the most important step was convincing important Freemen that Richard must be curbed, even if that meant interfering with The Way and the running of the Retreat Houses. With powerful ties of blood and marriage to many of the minor Houses, Harlan was still the strongest House, even though its lord was imprisoned and the vassals that held it in trusteeship for Council fought over every decision.

CHAPTER 12

At the last possible minute before departure, I fed Narra so she would sleep and not betray us with crying. Then Ennis, Narra, and I, and our ''picnic basket'' (filled mostly with Narra's necessities) went to the door. Ennis presented a pass, signed by the Odonnel physician, that allowed him to take the baby and me into the sunshine for Narra's health. (Everyone understood *I* was going along only as Narra's food supply.) Narra was a little yellow and would benefit from several hours in real sunlight, starting at dawn, the pass said. This was the debt Ennis had called in: the help of the physician.

I knew no baby should lie ''hours'' in the sun, but the soldiers didn't, and that would give us more time before our escape was discovered. The soldiers seemed to have difficulty even reading the pass. One suggested calling their superior officer for help. Ennis's hand, which rested on my waist, closed hard on my ribs, but his voice remained smooth and cool. He shrugged with apparent casualness.

''Your choice. I remember how much paperwork there is if a soldier leaves his post without orders to, but it is important that you handle this properly. Maybe you *should* call your captain.''

His words horrified me. They smacked of betrayal. I told myself Ennis couldn't be betraying us. He had to be gambling the soldiers wouldn't call their officer. I had to trust him. I *knew* he meant to get us free.

The older soldier looked at him, looked at his comrade, looked at the tips of his own boots. ''I don't reckon we have to do that. Dr. Alterinn must know what he's doing.'' His face twisted in thought. ''Could I see the baby?'' he finally hazarded. ''I have a little boy myself.''

I stepped closer and turned back the blanket from Narra's face. The soldier tickled her gently under the chin with a thick finger, a tickle gentle enough not to wake her up.

''She do look a little yellow,'' he said in a voice of experience. He stepped back and saluted Ennis. ''Good luck with the sunshine treatment, my lord.''

The hand at my waist relaxed and we walked casually down the corridor toward the lift.

Because we were ''sunning the baby,'' we could not leave by flitter. Ennis commed the chief groom from the lift shelter on the surface and told him to bring us two gentle horses. He had to show the groom the pass, too, before the man would let go of the horses. Ennis told him we were going to the hills at the south end of the lake to take advantage of the first rays of the sun, then we rode off. We would be crossing the boundary into Harlan Holding, but between allies that did not matter.

The hills around the lake were small, but large enough to hide us from anyone watching from the manor. As soon as we reached the shore of the lake, Ennis turned northeast. The shore was mostly sheets and slabs of lava, so the horses slipped and stumbled often, but we left no trail. After a short distance, Ennis stopped to look back. A little more of the tenseness left his body.

''Maybe we're really free,'' he said, almost to himself.

''You still think we'll be caught?''

He looked at me with shadowed eyes. ''It looks good now, but there are spies everywhere. You know that.''

I knew that. I'd always known that.

By mid-afternoon we reached the river that feeds Harlan's

big lake. Trees protected us from being spotted from overhead, so when we heard fliers at about fifteen hours, we didn't worry. At nightmeal time, we came to the east-west trade road through the plains and just south of the edge of the northern Frozen Zone. A caravan was proceeding slowly eastward along it. Ennis raised his arm and the man on the lead wagon stopped his horses. We rode up to him.

He was dark beyond how the Gharr are dark. This man had *black* hair, thinning on top, very curly below. His eyes were dark brown. His companion, otherwise of similar coloring, had blue eyes. He and Egil were the only blue-eyed people I had ever seen. Ennis and the driver exchanged no words, but the driver waved his hand toward the back of his wagon, slapped the reins across his horses' backs, and started up again. We fell in behind as directed.

We didn't travel far, as it was almost dark. When the caravan reached a wide meadow beside the road, the caravan master called the wagons into a circle. Everyone seemed to have an assigned task. Wagon drivers unhitched the horses and children led them to grass and hobbled them. Women gathered wood and started fires for cooking. Other women and girls crouched over large cloths spread on the ground, mixing ingredients for supper so that when the fires were hot, the food would be ready to cook.

That night, when Ennis and I lay together in the back of a wagon and talked, I learned these people were Gypsies. I'd never seen Gypsies before. They don't live in our part of the world much. Ennis said in the summer they traded, mostly in horses, and traveled. In winter, they lived in freecities, training horses, making jewelry (mostly the men), doing needlework (both men and women), or telling fortunes and reading palms (mostly the women) as Gypsies have done for thousands of years.

That night there was a disturbance outside the ring of wagons. Ennis looked out, but said he could see nothing. A short time afterward, the caravan master came to the wagon.

"You've been found, milord," the caravan master said. "We killed two of the men who attacked our sentries, but at least one escaped. We are not soldiers here, milord."

"I don't expect you to be. How did they get here?"

"On foot, as far as my men backtracked them. That means a flier of some sort, but it's too dark to track far without light. If these men are after you, milord, a light wouldn't be safe for anyone who got too near anyway. I want you out of my caravan, milord. As I said, we're not soldiers here and I only agreed to provide cover, not defense."

Ennis nodded. "I understood that. Let me talk to my wife a few minutes."

The caravan master walked several meters away from the wagon. Ennis turned to me. I wished I had light enough to see his face. I was terrified. I'd thought we'd gotten clean away, yet, somehow, we'd been followed. My mind spun. How many men were there? What could we do to save ourselves out in this wilderness? What could we do with no walls and no soldiers to protect us? I could never survive outside on the surface. All my life I'd had the security of stone walls over and around me. What would happen to us, to Narra after we were caught? Whose men? Odonnel's? Harlan's? Why—

Ennis was shaking me. "Don't fall apart on me now, Kathryn! Think! My guess is whoever's following us is after you. And maybe Narra. Me they can take care of any time."

He stopped and took a deep, unsteady breath. "I'm afraid, Kathryn, really afraid. We're out in the middle of nowhere with nothing but ourselves to rely on. The Gypsies were paid to let us join them, but Gypsies don't die for money. We're on our own. We've crossed Richard. We've embarrassed Garren. Either one of them could be ordering the men out there. If we're caught, we die. Or I die and you hurt a lot, maybe for a long time."

It was no comfort that his thoughts were so like my own. I clutched him so hard he winced. "The baby, Ennis. What if they want the baby?"

"Then they'll get her, eventually," he said bleakly. "I'll make that as hard for them as I can, though. We must separate."

My mind raced after that idea. If we could fool the pursuers into following only one of us . . . But there was nothing here but the caravan and the forest, or the plains to the south or the fringes of the Frozen Zone. I couldn't keep *myself* alive in any of those places, let alone a baby. I wished, for the first time since I was a child, that I'd been born male. Then I wouldn't be so ignorant of the outside.

"Kathryn!" Ennis said sharply. "Pay attention! I'll take Narra. You stay with the caravan."

"You take the baby?" That idea hadn't occurred to me and it jarred my thoughts into disorder. How could such a young baby go anywhere without her mother? "Where will you go? How will she eat? What will I do?" I hated the whimper in my voice, but I'd lived too long in my enemy's House not to be deathly afraid and I could not disguise or bury my feelings as Karne could.

Ennis bent his head until his forehead touched mine. I could feel his love for me in his touch. "The two of Halarek blood can't stay together. I'll do everything I can to save Narra, but you two *can't* stay together. And I can't tell you where I intend to go. What you don't know, you can't tell." He pulled me into his arms. "It will take a little while for me to get the equipment we'll need packed onto a horse. See if you can persuade Narra to eat. After that I'm afraid she'll have to live on water for a day or so."

I huddled against him. He might save Narra. A baby could live a day or so without milk, couldn't it? But surviving was going to be hard. Hard for Narra. Hard for Ennis. I didn't want to be separated from either of them, but he was right. With an enemy close, the two Halareks should *not* be together.

Ennis left before dawn began to lighten the sky. Narra had, the Guardians be thanked, nursed without complaint, so she was asleep when they left. Ennis had acquired a backboard to carry her in so his hands would be free. We hugged as if this were to be the last time and parted without words. On his orders, I didn't watch him go. It was a long time before I fell asleep.

Shouts, screams, and the sizzle of beamer bolts awakened me just after dawn. I stuck my head out the curtain at the back of the wagon. Across the circle, the wooden back door of a wagon was burning. Several women were throwing buckets of water on it. Outside the circle, men in Odonnel checks ran, dodged, knelt to shoot. The shooting was mostly for effect, since the Gypsies weren't resisting, and was soon over.

Garren Odonnel himself jumped his horse over a wagon

tongue and came into the center of the ring. He shouted imperiously for the caravan master. The master set down the bucket of water he had been carrying to one of the fires and came to Lharr Garren at once. The Lharr bent from his saddle to speak quietly to him. The master pointed toward my wagon. Garren rode toward me, calling several soldiers to him with a jerk of his head. I pulled my head back in, but not before I saw a squad of Odonnel soldiers on the other side of the circle dragging three Gypsy women away.

Odonnel pulled his horse up outside with a jingle of tack. "Ennis Harlan! Kathryn Halarek! I know you're in there. Come out!"

At least he didn't know yet Ennis had gone. I stuck my head out the back door and looked up at him. His face was hard and his eyes cold.

"My lord?" I managed to say.

"You and your husband have embarrassed my House. You'll both pay. Even Richard agrees that you'll pay. *Ennis* will *die*." His tone left worse possibilities for me. "Where's Ennis?"

"Ennis, my lord?" I tried to sound sleepy and confused.

"Yes, Ennis!" he snarled. He raised his head to look over mine. "Ennis! ENNIS! Get out here."

Ennis didn't come, of course.

"Where is he?"

"I—I don't know, my lord." I needed no acting for my voice to shake. I was glad Ennis and the baby had escaped, at least for now, but I knew who would take the consequences.

Garren grabbed me by the shoulders and hauled me half out of the wagon. "What do you mean, you don't know?"

"I don't know. He—he left in the night, milord."

Garren let go abruptly. I managed to catch myself on the edge of the lower door. Garren rode to the edge of the circle and began shouting to the men outside. He was too angry and too far away for me to understand what he said beyond a general demand to FIND ENNIS. I crept back into the wagon and sat down on a mound of bedding behind the driver's seat. I rolled a shirt into a blanket so, from a distance, such as the back of the wagon, the bundle would look like a swaddled infant. Stalling was all I had left. I cuddled the bundle as if nursing and prayed for the safety of Ennis and Narra. I knew there would be none for me.

Garren was at the tailgate again. "Come here, Kathryn," he ordered.

"I'm feeding the ba—"

Garren leaped from his horse and lunged the length of the wagon. He grabbed me by the knot of hair at the back of my neck and dragged me to the tailgate. He jumped to the ground, ripped the bundle from me and dropped it on the ground, then pulled me after him with a jerk. I landed hard. I wondered if he knew the bundle was empty. I wondered if it mattered to him if there were a baby in it. Before I could get my breath back, Garren's boot landed in my rib.

"Where is he?" He kicked me again.

I felt a rib give. It hurt. A lot. My next breath came with stabbing pain. "Does Richard accept damaged goods, mi-lord?" I gasped.

That stopped him with his boot drawn back.

"I thought not." For this remark, too, I would pay, but while Garren was angry and thinking about me or about Richard, he couldn't put his mind to where Ennis would be likely to hide.

Odonnel jerked me to my feet. "There can be pain without visible damage, Lady Kathryn." His voice was as deadly as a wind in Uhl.

My mouth went dry with fear. Odonnel shoved me ahead of him into the center of the fire circle and motioned two soldiers to hold me. He demonstrated extensively just how much pain there could be without visible damage. I struggled, I pleaded, I promised to do anything he wanted, *give* him anything he wanted if he would just stop. But he would not stop. If I had known where Ennis had gone, I would have betrayed him. I screamed and screamed until my throat could no longer make a sound, then I could bear no more and passed out. Odonnel had me roused and made one last try to get information he must have known I didn't have, but the sport seemed to be gone once his victim could not even sit up by herself. I passed out again.

I awakened to a swaying motion. My stomach rolled un-pleasantly to match it. I opened my eyes. The roof overhead was curved, dark-blue, and painted with the constellations and the moon. This was not my wagon. The greased-leather curtains over the opening beyond my feet let sunlight in through a gap between the curtains' center edges and also through a space where a nail, which was supposed to hold the curtain to the curve of the roof, had fallen out. The light revealed boxes stacked across the end under the curtain, a net of garlic hanging from the ceiling, and a jumble of clothes, rain gear, fishing poles, lanterns, boxes of staples like salt and flour, and bedding. It smelled of oil, smoke, spices, garlic, and dust.

Outside, several uleks lowed. That meant this wagon was at the rear of the caravan, where the herd was. Wheels rumbled over the dirt road and dust from them powdered everything, even my skin, with a gritty film. A dog barked. Two men's voices, somewhere behind and slightly above my head, discussed the weather and the road. I thought about rolling over and asking the men to stop the wagon before the smells and the swaying made me throw up all over its inside. After a while, I tried to reach them, but the attempt hurt so much and made me feel so sick that I lay back as I had been with a moan. My throat felt dry. My head hurt abominably. Every part of my body hurt abominably.

Behind my head, what was probably another leather curtain from the sound of it was pushed out of the way. A young woman came through it and sat down beside me.

"I'm going to be sick," I told her.

The young woman shook her head, pointed to my mouth, and mimed drinking from a cup. I wasn't at all sure that was the right thing to do at the moment, but I couldn't move without help. The young woman dipped a ladle of water for me out of a lidded bucket near my head. After she had set the lid back on the bucket, she helped me lift my head, then held the ladle to my lips. I drained it. She dipped more water and I drank that, too. From my mouth's dryness, I guessed I'd been unconscious quite a long time. I did feel better. Perhaps the nausea had been from having my eyes shut while the wagon was moving.

I looked at the young woman. "Thank you. I do feel better."

She nodded and smiled.

"Where are we going?" My voice, watered, was less scratchy and hoarse now.

She shrugged.

"How long have I been out?"

She held up two fingers.

"Two days?"

She nodded vigorously.

"Don't you speak Rom?" It was said Gypsies had their own language, but even if that were so, people can still sometimes understand much of what is said in a language they're used to hearing without being able to speak it.

She looked at me, puzzled for a moment, then nodded, then shook her head and pointed to her ears, then nodded again. She knew Rom! I felt a weak elation. My head, though it continued to hurt like nothing I'd experienced before, still worked. Then the young woman turned toward the light, opened her mouth, and pointed. Even in the dimness of the wagon, I could see she had only a stub where her tongue had been. She looked very sad for a moment, then her face turned angry and she flung herself toward the back of the wagon, flipped open the curtain and hooked a ring on it over a hook on the doorway. She pointed a rigid finger at the soldiers riding behind and beside the wagon. They were wearing Freemen's sarks and hosen, but on this warm day they had left the sarks open at the neck and the Odonnel checks underneath showed. They would look harmless from the air, though, members of a mixed caravan of Gharr merchants and Gypsies. The young woman motioned *taller*, then pointed to a red scarf dangling from a nail near the rear opening.

"Someone in Odonnel did that? Someone taller, with red on?"

She nodded to the first two questions, but shook her head at the third and patted her hair, almost pounded it.

"Someone with red in his hair?"

She nodded vigorously.

"Lharr Garren Odonnel?"

She nodded until I thought her head might come off.

"But why?"

Her hands flashed, signing something, but I couldn't understand. She saw I didn't understand and quit in mid-motion.

She turned and began digging vigorously through the clothes and bedding near my feet. Eventually she dug out a tablet and a pencil. She sat in front of me with her legs crossed tailor fashion and her back mostly to me, so I could read over her shoulder, and began writing swiftly, using her knee as support for the tablet. That she could write surprised me. I'd always assumed Gypsies were illiterate.

The words on the tablet said: "I was working in a jeweler's shop in Erinn last winter. I was unlucky enough to pass an alley where Garren Odonnel was strangling one of his mistresses. I did not know who he was at first, or I would not have interfered, but I heard a woman screaming for help, so I took my knife"—here she paused to pull a knife rather dramatically from a sheath on her thigh—"and ran into the alley to help her. Odonnel had finished her before I arrived. His companions took her body from his hands while I watched. He would have killed me, too, right then. An alley murder is not something even a lord of the Nine wants anyone else to know about. His companions reminded him I was Gypsy and that if he killed me, my family would no longer deal with his House."

She looked over her shoulder at me, fire in her eyes. I could see how frustrated she was at having to tell all this with a pencil instead of her voice. Then she bent to the paper again.

"They were right. My family would no more have carried his goods on the summer caravans afterward than they could fly to the moon. They would not have brought him the trade goods from the south he so desires, either. No Gypsy caravan would have. So he had his companions tie me up. They smuggled me out of the city, because Odonnel had no charge to try me with in Freemen's court and because I could speak against him. The companions took me to Erinn manor and the manor court. They accused me falsely of spying and Garren Odonnel sentenced me to have my tongue cut out."

She stopped writing for a time with her head hanging down. I saw a spot on the paper darken because a tear touched it and then another. She took a deep breath with a little sob in it and continued writing.

"He thought his story would be safe. Everyone knows Gypsies can't read or write. There he underestimated us. He also overestimated a Gypsy's love of profit. He would have done as well to kill me, because our entire clan vowed never to work for Odonnel or his vassals again because of what he did to me."

She looked at me with grim satisfaction. I nodded.

"So how do you come to be working for Odonnel now? I would've thought your family would never—"

She snatched the tablet from me and wrote furiously. "Harlan soldiers captured my mother and two aunts. If we do not carry you safe to Breven, they will be killed. This is the Duke of Harlan's plan. The Odonnel men are only minions here."

"And you trust Harlan to keep his word?"

She shrugged, then wrote: "What have we to lose? If our women die, Odonnel and Harlan men die also, as they deserve to. We have serf friends in their Houses. A drop of poison in wine and it is all over. Your people are not familiar with poison. They will never suspect."

I shivered. The Gypsies were apparently as thirsty for revenge as the Gharr, but they were cleverer and more subtle about it. I shut my eyes, exhausted by the effort of even so brief a conversation, and was almost immediately asleep again.

The caravan progressed slowly toward Breven. I progressed very slowly back toward health, though Garren had been correct in saying he would do no permanent damage. By listening to what the Gypsies called her, I learned the young woman's name, which was Miri or something close to that. I also picked up the basic hand signs with which Miri communicated, because her hands talked far faster than her pencil. I had nothing else to do but worry about Ennis and Narra. There was nothing to read and I was not allowed out of the wagon when the caravan stopped to trade—at the horse fair the men had been talking about, and then for a delivery to House Kath, and then . . .

As soon as I could move about a little, I learned one reason I'd been given to the care of the Gypsies rather than to the troop of soldiers—to keep me from the soldiers' lecherous hands. I once heard two Odonnel soldiers, who were riding right beside my wagon, discussing what fun it would be to beat the mighty Duke of Harlan to my bed. They were lucky they worked for Odonnel. Such stupidity wouldn't have survived

long in Harlan. Several times soldiers did try to crawl into my
wagon, only to have Miri's father chase them off with a whip.
One, whom the whip did not convince, died with his head
inside the curtain and a knife in his back. The Gypsies dumped
his body into a ravine, then pushed rocks down on it, as if he
had died in a slide, or so Miri told me. Several soldiers also
made attempts on Miri, who slept in the next wagon. She
quickly dissuaded them with her knife.

The soldiers' attempts to get at me made me think of what
waited at Breven and so, for the most part, I kept my thoughts
on the Gypsies and how they lived. To think of Breven was
to despair. I couldn't escape whatever Richard had planned for
me. Even now, when I was in the open and rescue was possible,
I wouldn't be rescued. Karne or Nik could never find me in a
caravan because there were so many Gild and merchant caravans on the roads this time of year. That was why Ennis had
planned this method of travel. Even if there hadn't been dozens
of caravans, few people, including my brother, would consider
a Gypsy caravan as a hiding place, because Gypsies, though
rare, are so conspicuous.

Late one sunny afternoon in Aden, we finally reached
Breven. The caravan stopped outside the forest of bluepines
that surrounds the Retreat House, and the caravan master ordered the wagons pulled into a circle. The Odonnel sergeant
shouted at him to stay put if he wanted his women back, then
ordered his men to get their horses and their butts onto the
troop transport and pointed. I could see the top half of the
transport rising above a swell in the ground. The soldiers left
quickly.

Gypsy men with gunpowder weapons and arrows and knives
and some stunners came immediately from wagon seats and
horse-holding to guard the openings between wagons. The
women and children and uleks stayed in the open center. The
Gypsies didn't set up fires or unharness the horses as had been
usual at day's end. Children held the horses, and all the women
had weapons of some sort close at hand. The caravan master
sent a boy in to the abbot to announce the Gypsies's arrival.

After a time, soldiers in Harlan green came out of the trees,
dragging three women in gypsy colors after them. Even from
a distance, I could see the women were a lot worse for their

time with Harlan. The caravan master and Miri's father and the other men saw, too, and gathered quickly to talk in murmurs.

"Bring out the Halarek woman," the man at the fore of the Harlan soldiers shouted.

They did not even have the decency to use my title.

Miri's father led me to the nearest opening, but he held me back from stepping over the wagon tongue. "She is here. Send us our women first, that we may see that they *are* our women."

The soldiers came closer and several drew weapons. The women lifted battered faces to be recognized. One of them limped badly, one cradled what looked like a broken arm, the third had to be supported by two soldiers. A growl from the Gypsy men rumbled around the circle. I shivered. Could Richard, or his commander out here, also have underestimated them? Odonnel's men certainly had.

"We did not give permission for them to be used by your rabble," the wagon master snarled.

The Harlan leader tossed his head. "We agreed only to return them alive if the Halarek woman arrived alive. My men here have been without women for far too long to—"

He died in his arrogance. An arrow took him in the throat. The soldiers stood a moment in stunned amazement. It had been centuries since arrows had been used in battle. In that moment, a mob of children broke from the circle of wagons, swarmed around the women like ants, and carried them swiftly back inside the circle while stunner fire laid all the remaining soldiers on the ground. The moment the children and their burdens were safely inside, the men leaped over the wagon tongues and slit the throats of the Harlan soldiers.

"Saves bullets and arrows for another day," Miri's father told me.

Miri mimed that the men had used stunners so if children were hit accidentally, no damage would be done.

I, too, felt stunned. This was war as I had never seen it. No chivalry, no pride in "honorable" versus "dishonorable" ways to kill the enemy. If the enemy was to die, it was best done efficiently and with as few losses of men and weapons as could be managed. The tactics had been brilliant. The Gypsies had been outgunned, yet Harlan men had died without knowing what hit them. Even as the captives were being splinted and bandaged and comforted, the men were taking the horses's heads and leading them and their wagons out of the circle.

Miri's father came to my side. "It is my sorrow that we must leave you here with these iniquitous people, my lady, but we made an agreement: you delivered here in return for our women delivered to us. Though it is our right, we will not abuse you as our women have been abused. We have kept you safe from such treatment, but we can protect you no longer."

He pointed north through the bluepines. "Breven is there. If you lose yourself for several hours, it would be of enormous help to us. In three or four hours, we can disappear into the Frozen Zone. It is summer. We can live there long enough for any hunt to die down." He lifted his hands in a who-knows gesture. "Perhaps we are not important enough to the great lords to be hunted at all, but we will not take that chance." He turned away and began shouting orders in his own language to a clump of older boys who had been hovering just out of hearing.

I turned to Miri to tell her goodbye. She had been kind. Tears made her cheeks glisten. She hugged me quickly and then ran to her wagon and climbed in.

I stepped over a wagon tongue and left the Gypsies behind. I could wander in the woods, Miri's father had said. I could certainly do that, especially if it would help them get away. I could even make tracking me difficult. I owed the Gypsies at least that much just for keeping the soldiers off me.

The air among the bluepines was cooler than it was in the late afternoon sunlight, and was fragrant with pine and water. Birds twittered and whispered to each other above and around me. Ahead and to my right I heard a gull. A gull's cry meant Lake St. Paul was in that direction. I imagined the slow lapping of waves on gravel. My soul needed the quiet such could bring.

I broke a long, supple branch from a tree and tied it to the back of my belt, where its needles would brush out my tracks. It would leave a trail of fine grooves, obviously made in an unnatural manner, but trackers would have to guess *who* had wanted to conceal a trail. It would be dusk soon, and that, too, would slow searchers. If I were clever, and careful, I would have time to sit alone and listen to the lake for a time before someone from the Retreat House found me.

Eventually a commotion began behind me as men from Breven, perhaps come out to learn what was keeping the first squad of soldiers, discovered soldiers dead and Gypsies and "the Halarek woman" gone. Perhaps they would chase the Gypsies a distance, thinking they had taken me with them. No, there were footprints from the remains of the circle to the place where I cut the branch. Any sort of tracker at all would draw the correct conclusion. Because the soldiers didn't follow me at once, I had to assume they had no such tracker with them.

I wound in circles and spirals through the trees for an hour or so, then went to the lakeshore and sat on a flat, warm rock in a little bay. The lake had the fresh smell of open water. Young bluepines hid me from the Retreat House. A light wind soughed through their needles and blew the slightly dusty smell of wet rocks to me. The waves lapped as gently on the fine gravel beach as I'd imagined they would. To my left, some small animal splashed in the water. There was a much bigger splash, an anguished yelp, and the shore was quiet again.

That's me, I thought, waiting by the shore for the stronger animal to get me.

I looked down the lake to its end. A few white lights marked the lift shelters and com dishes of the freecity of Loch. It was summer. Loch was only twenty or so kilometers away. I could walk there and be taken in, safe from Richard. But inertia had set in. My experiences at Garren Odonnel's hands had beaten me. I didn't really believe I could walk to the city. Physically I had healed enough, but my mind kept saying, "What's the use? Richard will get you in the end."

I stood anyway. I made myself take one step and then another and another along the shore toward Loch.

There's no rescue, an insidious voice in my mind said. *Karne can't find you. Nik can't find you. Loch will just give you back. Richard is too strong.* My body felt heavy and very reluctant.

Men's voices rang through the woods. I reminded myself of Adrian's optimism and confidence in herself. If a Freewoman could be strong like that, a woman of the Nine certainly could. I turned toward the city again, but I had waited too long. Torchlight splashed in thin white lines through the trees. I ran.

The gravel made my feet slide back for every step I took. Torches cast brilliant white light and stark shadows behind and ahead of me. I dodged into the woods. Going would be slower there, but I'd be harder to find among the trees and their shadows. Men crashed through the underbrush behind and then ahead of and then beside me, stumbling over exposed roots or rocks, cursing, but slowly surrounding me. I learned then how a rabbit feels when the dogs close in. In moments, men in green Harlan uniforms made a hostile circle around me from which I could not escape.

CHAPTER 13

Late at night on 40 Aza, Karne stumbled into Ontar's personal-family dining room. Nik and Orkonan were playing a game of chess beside the remains of their nightmeal. Orkonan looked up.

"How did it go?"

Karne sank into a chair with a weary sigh. "So-so. Call up some food for me, will you?" He crossed his arms on the table and laid his head on them. Within seconds he was asleep, the voices of his friends coming to him like dim echoes through a fog.

"Should I wake him, Nik?"

A chess piece clicked against the board.

"If he's run today like he has most of the others, he hasn't had anything to eat since morning."

Karne drifted farther away. Gentle shaking brought him partway back, then less gentle shaking. Karne's head came up slowly. He looked at Orkonan, who kept fading in and out of focus.

"Wha' do you wan', Tane?" he said and tried to lay his heavy head back down.

Orkonan gripped Karne's shoulder more firmly. "Your meal, Karne."

"Wha'? Oh."

Orkonan lifted a lid and the scent of roasted meat drifted out. Karne sniffed appreciatively and pushed his body slowly erect.

"Haven't eaten since last night," he mumbled.

Nik and Orkonan exchanged a look Karne told himself he ought to understand, but he did not. Tonight his lack of understanding did not bother him. He reached a slow hand toward the uncovered dish. Orkonan sat down again at the chessboard and resumed the game.

When Karne at last pushed back his plate and sighed, Orkonan looked up from the chessboard. "How did it go today?"

The question seemed vaguely familiar. Had Orkonan asked him that before? "So-so. Sindt of Durlin finally, in as surly a way as he could manage, agreed to vote with me. Add Arlen of Koort and it may be enough. If the Freemen see sense."

Orkonan kept one eye on the board as he spoke. "Tell us whatever other news you have in the morning, Karne. You're dead on your feet."

"On his seat, you mean." Nik dodged a mock blow from Orkonan's fist.

"Spoken like my old tutor," Karne said with a tired smile. He stood slowly, checked around him to be sure he had not left anything, and headed toward the door.

He fell into his bed without even undressing, but thoughts of the months and months of meetings and parties and social calls and even bribes it had taken to put together a very fragile coalition kept him awake for some time. With House Durlin added to the roster, there had to be enough votes. There *had* to be.

Someone rapped cautiously on the outer door.

Karne lifted his head. The chrono beside the bed said it was morning already. Late morning. It did not feel like morning to him. The knocking became more urgent.

"Come," he said grudgingly.

Orkonan came in only as far as the inner doorjamb, Nik right behind him. Nik's face was alight with excitement.

"Tri-d announcement just came through from Lady Agnes,

milord," Orkonan said. "Lord Ennis and Lady Kathryn escaped Odonnel with the baby two days ago."

"Escaped". The word hit Karne like a bomb. For a moment he could not even remember what the word meant, because it was so unbelievable. Ennis Harlan had helped Kit Halarek escape Richard's control? And the baby, too. He had taken the baby even though Richard's plans for Halarek required a half-blooded child? Karne shook his head, unbelieving. "Are you sure?"

"Have you ever known Lady Agnes to lie?" Orkonan asked dryly. "She saw them walk out past the guards."

Karne did not let himself get his hopes up. He could not afford to. Maybe they had left their quarters freely, but they could have been recaptured before they reached the end of the first hall. He rolled over and sat up, then ran his hands through his hair several times to wake himself up more. "Did she say where they went?"

"She didn't know, milord. Safest thing would've been to hook up with a caravan somewhere."

Nik, who had been bursting to say something, finally could restrain himself no longer. "I checked with Uncle Emil. Our spies in Erinn report Ennis took horses."

"Smart." Karne was completely awake now. "Flitters are too easy to find and too easy to shoot down." He felt a grudging admiration for this unwanted brother-in-law who was defying his head-of-House. Ennis had to know what would happen to him should Richard find him. "Call Wynter," he ordered, looking at Orkonan. "We'll meet him in the library."

Orkonan went to the call box near the door to the Larga's quarters. Karne headed for the stair to the library, with Nik on his heels. Nik's boyish eagerness had begun to worry him. That quality made him a daring pilot, but it would make him a very poor commanding officer. Karne had only seconds to figure out how to handle the problems that made. Nik was the Heir of a close ally and would be commanding the von Schuss forces in any attack on a stronghold that held Kit.

By the time his feet hit the library floor, Karne decided to use Wynter's military experience as grounds for making him coordinator of the allied forces. That way, any rash plan Nik came up with would affect only Nik.

Karne sat at the worktable. Orkonan took his place on Karne's left, prepared to take notes or send messages as necessary. Nik and Wynter sat across from them. Karne looked at Wynter.

"Ennis Harlan got Kit out of Odonnel somehow, General. I brought the three of you here to ask your advice about the best way to find them before Richard's men do. I'd thought of sending up fliers, which would be quick, but we have the western half of a world to search. Ground search, except along Harlan's boundary, would be even more fruitless."

"Get Gild satellite pix," said Wynter. "If they reveal anything possibly useful, start a ground search in that area."

"Are Gild pix able to show anything as small as two horses?" Nik sounded impatient. "Use our spy networks, Karne. Ours, yours, Duval's, our vassals' (if you have any vassals you'd trust with the information). Then, when we know definitely what area to search, we can use the other methods."

In spite of Nik's impatience and Wynter's matter-of-factness, Karne felt excitement building. Kit was out above ground! She could be found, rescued. Talking about it made it seem more real. "We'll tell some of the minor Houses what's happened, too, not just the spies. Houses Konnor and Koort, certainly. And Durlin, because of Netta and the boys."

"House Arnette?" Orkonan suggested, with a lift of one eyebrow.

Karne gave a contemptuous snort. "Lord Francis might have stayed loyal if Lizanne had lived, if only for appearances, but nothing ties him to me now. No, never Arnette."

"DeVree, of course."

Nik nodded. "If not for Kit, then against Richard."

"Van McNeece," Orkonan put in. "If anyone wants Richard controlled, he does."

The men discussed the who and how. They went over the list of who was to be told Kit had escaped, then checking it and double checking it. There weren't many names, compared to the number of Houses in Council, but it was a much longer list than Karne could have gathered even a year before. In his first political fight with Richard four years earlier, only House von Schuss, House McNeece, House Konnor, and House Justin had stood with him. Thinking of the discussion that had led to this list, Karne felt a little more confident about Council. If these Houses could be trusted with this information, they would stand with him on 15 Aden, too.

General Wynter looked at the list, then at his lord. He shook his head. "The spy network's the best way to spread such a message, milord, even to these other Houses. It's a little slower than messengers, but messengers are highly visible and too many are bribable. Spies are a lot more secure. They know who spies for the enemy in whose Houses." His mouth quirked upward. "The only faster method, they say, is to tell a waiting-woman, milord."

Karne nodded agreement. "We could get lucky. Ennis and his family might show up at some neutral or friendly House and make a search unnecessary." Deep inside, Karne believed that was too much to hope for. It would be too easy and nothing on Starker IV came easily. Karne did not have to look at a map to see how much territory Ennis would have to lead his family through before they were off either Odonnel or Harlan Holding.

"We can pray for their safety," he said at last. "There's no way to help them until they leave Harlan Holding. There's no way to help them until we find them."

The spy network was set to work. Wynter organized ground search units of Blues for Halarek's border areas and Specials for the areas just outside the Harlan boundary. Baron von Schuss did the same for his holding. The soldiers questioned everyone coming out of either Harlan or Odonnel about what they had seen there. The patrols in place, Nik flew home to confer with his uncle. Karne flew to deVree Holding to talk to the duke.

On his way home, Karne detoured past Durlin to see if Netta's brother Sindt was maintaining a strict guard, both of his holding's perimeter and of his manor house. He was not, and nothing Karne said could convince him that a man imprisoned at Breven, half a world away, was a danger to his nephews. Worse, Sindt's blind stubbornness made Karne's own lack of heirs even more serious, because even an incompetent assassin would have no trouble entering Sindt's manor. Richard hired no incompetents.

Karne took off from Durlin Holding reminding himself to

ask Orkonan as soon as he got back about the search for a new Larga. Then a skip-cast blasted into the flier's cabin on the secured channel.

"Urgent request. Stop at McNeece Holding. Urgent request. Stop at McNeece Holding." The tech at Ontar had apparently repeated the message so often that his voice had gone monotone and machinelike.

Karne leaned a little toward the control panel so his voice would be picked up as clearly as possible. "Message received and accepted." He set the com to repeat that message automatically and corrected his course toward McNeece.

What could Van want that he would describe as urgent? Had something happened to Van and his wife needed help? Had McNeece Holding been attacked? Why no more information? Karne was beginning to feel the effects of a very long day, with what was shaping up to be a long night still ahead. Karne set his flitter down on the McNeece flitter pad with the abruptness of which Kit and Nik both often complained. The pad showed no sign of invasion. When the heat of the flitter's exhaust had dissipated, Van McNeece himself stepped out from behind the blast shield. Karne felt secure, then, in stepping out of the flitter and hopping down onto the pad. Enemy attack, at least, was not the emergency. McNeece motioned him through the pad door into the adjoining hall. A man stood resting the back of his head against the far wall, his eyes closed. He was holding a baby against his shoulder. Only the baby's wide-eyed, curious face watched Karne. The man was Ennis Harlan. Karne suppressed the reflexive reach for his stunner only with difficulty; Ennis was in Van's manor and was not under guard.

"You see why I could tell you nothing?" Van asked. "I commed you as soon as he arrived."

"Thanks," Karne said. "I'll remember."

Karne turned to Ennis. The man was pale, but he stood straight and quiet while Karne looked him up and down. Karne made no effort to conceal his hostility. This man had taken Kit against her will, ancient custom or not. He had killed hundreds to do it. "Where's Kit?" he barked.

Ennis stiffened, but he met Karne's eyes squarely. "Lord Richard wants to get a child by her. I thought we'd eluded him, but we hadn't. His men attacked the Gypsy caravan we'd joined. The Gypsies stopped that first attack, but Kit and I decided it was best to split up before reinforcements came. No matter which trail the attackers followed after that, half the Halarek females would be safe. I took Narra.''

Karne felt some of the hostility leave him. Ennis had acted to save his child and his wife from his own head-of-House. Only a very brave man would do that. ''Richard may not have been after your blood literally before, but he will be now,'' Karne said dryly.

''I know.'' Ennis's voice was steady and so were his eyes. ''But you and McNeece and your allies can protect Narra.'' His voice broke then and he shifted the baby, then bent his head to look at her.

Likely to conceal a tear, too, that move, Karne thought. He knows he won't survive betraying Richard, especially not after betraying him twice—taking both the child he'd planned to control and the woman he wanted.

Ennis trailed his forefinger down the baby's cheek. ''I was selected as Kit's mate because my personal family breeds more girls resistant to the Sickness.'' He looked at Karne again. ''Believe me, my lord, I had no idea how Richard planned to get me a wife. Had I known, I'd never have agreed to such slaughter. Not that my disagreement would've made Richard any difference,'' he added rather bitterly. He took a deep breath. ''I've come to love your sister, my lord. I admire her courage and good sense. I'd give my life to spare her the indignities Richard intends for her, but if I gave my life trying to save her, who'd save Narra?''

Karne could see the man's anguish and hear it in his voice. It was a sign of the depth of his feelings that he mentioned them at all. Baring his soul that way meant he wanted something. A man did not expose himself like that, especially to strangers and enemies, unless he thought it might get him something he wanted very, very badly. Ennis gathered his courage almost visibly.

''McNeece, I ask you to take Narra into your care. I know how strongly you hate my House. Keep her safe to spite Richard. Keep her safe to help your friend Halarek. But keep her safe. Please.''

McNeece did not even glance at Karne. "In return for?"

"Giving me transport to Breven. I may yet be able to get Kathryn back."

"Don't be a fool, man!" McNeece growled. "Your life's not worth a wom's gizzard anywhere Harlan can reach you."

Ennis gripped McNeece's upper arm with his free hand. "She's my *wife!* Richard's going to hurt her!"

Hearing the roughness of her father's voice, or perhaps sensing his fear, Narra began to wail. Ennis released McNeece to console her. McNeece looked bewildered.

"She's just your wife," he said, uncomprehending. "It's not for you like it is for Karne. *You* can get heirs on any other woman. Halarek has only Karne and Lady Kathryn in direct line. And the two little boys. This is not a time for little boys and their regents."

Karne touched McNeece's arm and he quit talking. Clearly matters were for Ennis as they were for Nik: both men were too emotional about a woman and that impaired their thinking. "I'll send people to Breven at once," Karne said. "I'll go myself. You must stay here. You're the only legal protection Narra has until Kit's freed. If we fail, you're her only protection, period. Think! What can one man do against Richard and his soldiers?"

The question did not need to be answered.

After a time Ennis said, almost inaudibly, "I've been the cause of so much pain and loss for her already. This is too much."

"I don't intend Richard to have her," Karne responded grimly. "How did you escape and where did you last see Kit?"

Ennis quickly summarized the escape and meeting with the caravan.

"Good," Karne said. "Van, the use of your com room."

McNeece tapped the code into the locked door and it swung open. Karne strode into the room, ordered the techs to set a secure channel for Ontar, and mentally composed his message while the techs worked. Ennis had provided the clinching argument for Council: Richard intended to impugn the inheritance of Ennis's second child by begetting it, but forcing Ennis to claim it. This violated the Houses' most basic laws of inheritance—the laws that imposed faithfulness on a wife and prohibited stealing or using another man's legal wife. The adultery would also violate the Freemen's most precious moral standards. Ennis had the information that would seal Richard into a solitary room. Ennis should speak to Council, if he lives to speak to Council . . .

Just then Orkonan's sleep-wrinkled face appeared on the trid screen. "Sorry to wake you, Tane," Karne said. "Call Wynter, too. I want him to hear."

In a few minutes Wynter appeared. Karne beckoned Ennis into the room and asked him to tell his story and describe the caravan and the last place he had seen it. Ennis did so without protest. Wynter took notes and Karne could almost see the general's mental wheels going around, plotting a course and a speed for the caravan headed for Breven from Odonnel. Karne ordered Orkonan to set Weisman looking among the old maps and other documents to discover what, if anything, was known about the ruins east of Breven and the tunnels under the Retreat House.

"Wynter, assemble an attack force now. Specials only, I think. I'll be home in a few hours to check out what you've done," Karne said and signed off.

Karne then commed the Gild and asked for satellite pix of caravans in the northwest quadrant over the last week. Such requests were common and the Gild did not consider them violations of its neutrality. Pix were an ordinary part of the services the Gild offered its client worlds. However, there were so many caravans in summer that satellite pix had only limited value.

The essentials taken care of, Karne thanked McNeece and left the com room. He turned to the clearly exhausted man. "Forget attacking Breven single-handedly. You'd do Kit more good as a witness in Council. You'll live longer, too. Long enough to make a home for the three of you, perhaps." That thought stung, because of Nik, but Ennis deserved credit and help for the great courage he had shown. "Will you speak to Council of what happened to you and Kit?"

Ennis's smile was wry and weary. "Why not? I've already signed my own death warrant." The smile vanished. "I'd like to know I'd done something to at least slow Richard down. I didn't know how bad things were inside Harlan until I saw what was happening through Kathryn's eyes.''

"Come," McNeece said to Ennis in a kinder voice than he had used so far. ''You're done in. Let me take the baby. The Guardians know I've had enough of my own. I ordered up hot food when Karne announced he was coming in, so it'll be ready. Then you can sleep.'' McNeece motioned forward three of the soldiers who had been waiting farther down the hall. ''Guard this man. There may be assassins on the way.'' To Ennis he said, ''With your permission, and Karne's, of course, I'll send Narra somewhere absolutely safe, a place only Chairman Gashen and I will know about.''

Karne had seen Ennis's reluctance to hand over his daughter, to let her not only out of his arms but out of his knowledge. His emotions played across his face like shadows. At last Ennis said heavily, ''If she'll truly be safe.''

''As safe as anyone can be on Starker IV,'' McNeece promised. ''I have two girls of my own, you know, and one of them not yet a year older than your little one. If you survive your bout with Richard, you'll get her back. Or you and Lady Kathryn may decide to leave her in hiding until Karne has an heir of his own.''

Karne looked sharply at McNeece, but the man appeared to be speaking truth as he saw it; there was no implied insult about Karne's childlessness.

I'm getting too sensitive about this, Karne told himself.

Ennis handed Van the baby. McNeece set her in the crook of his left arm, which cradled her automatically, securely, and easily. ''Karne, this little one's an heir in your House, too. Have I your agreement also to send her to safety?''

Karne thought of the spies in Halarek, especially the deep spy who had fomented the rebellion at Farm 3. He thought of assassins, of sieges, even of the flight back to Ontar. The dangers in Halarek were many, too many when safety was offered elsewhere. ''You'll have my eternal gratitude, Van. If I don't have to worry about her, I can serve my House better.''

''Good.'' McNeece gave the baby's soft hair a quick stroke, then walked faster down the hall toward the lifts and his manor's main living areas. He glanced at the shorter Ennis. ''You've kept her in excellent condition, considering she's been away from her mother three days. How'd you do it?''

"Ulek milk the first day. From the Gypsies. Water yesterday and today.''

"My wife has what the little one needs. She can nurse two—ours and yours—for a few days.''

On the second level, McNeece handed Narra to a nursemaid, who was waiting at the entrance of the Great Hall to take her, then led the way to steaming meat, bread, and klag. Karne left McNeece Holding almost immediately after eating, and over Van's protests. There was no danger flying into Ontar after dark if the manor knew he was coming, and it did.

Once home, he snatched a few hours sleep, then called his allies for a conference. Karne decided to tell no one but Nik and Orkonan that Ennis was his source of information. He would only say that Kit had been located in a Gypsy caravan headed north. That would be enough. All his allies had daughters or sisters old enough to be stolen, should that old custom be successfully revived. Plans must be made now so there was no delay when someone found the Gypsy caravan.

There were several sightings of Gypsies in the southern hemisphere after that. In the first week of Aden, Konnor techs studying Gild satellite pix found Gypsies on a caravan road that could take them to Breven. When the Gypsies turned onto the Breven road, Karne and his officers met in the library to settle the final details for recovering Kit.

Nik, just returned from von Schuss Holding, joined the conference a few minutes after it started. His first question, before he had even shut the door was, "You've found her?" He sat down across the table from Karne. "I sure hope so. Our fliers are packed for battle.''

Karne looked at his friend. He nodded. "A Gypsy caravan's headed toward Breven. It's been a long wait, but it looks like our information about Richard's plans was accurate.''

Nik began swearing under his breath. Yan Willem said something foul about Richard's character and personal habits.

Weisman looked a little sick. "I would have thought this sort of depravity outside even Lord Richard's moral standards,'' he said.

"What about Ennis Harlan?" Dennen asked. "Are you telling him?"

"Ennis will be lucky to be alive next week," Karne said bluntly. "He got Kit out, and I owe him for that, but he's not with her now and I must protect Kit first. If I can. Ennis is going to have to fend for himself. I had Wynter gather the two troops of Specials he's prepared for this. We leave for Breven as soon as this meeting's over. Will von Schuss"—he looked at Nik—"and Justin"—he looked at Yan and Dennen—"support me?"

"Von Schuss has some men here already," Nik said. "Came with me. The rest will come when called by a prearranged signal."

"Good," Karne said. "I need that kind of support."

"The earl is most reluctant to act publicly," Dennen said with visible reluctance. "He does have a spy in Breven, though."

"So do we," said Nik.

"Sarcasm isn't necessary," Dennen snapped. "What that means is, the earl *is* willing to send a squad of his best undercover men, as soon as you ask, for whatever use you have, but no one in Justin colors."

Karne shook his head. "There's no way to tell friends from enemies out of uniform. I don't have so many friends that I can afford to kill any, so that's an offer I'm going to have to pass up."

"How soon do we leave?"

Karne looked at Nik. Even though Kit was someone else's wife, Nik was still eager to find her. Brinnd had been right. Karne looked at the others. "I figure if we arrive ahead of the caravan, Richard will know we've learned his plans and will change them so Kit won't be brought to Breven. He wouldn't be Richard if he didn't have a handful of alternative plans."

"How can we possibly prevent him from hurting her if we're not there first?" Nik's fear revealed itself in the roughness of his voice.

"We make several no-fire camps in the forest west of Loch. That way, we can reach Breven in minutes after one of the spies warns us the caravan's arrived."

"Won't Loch betray you?"

"Not if they don't know we're there, Tane."

Wynter rose. "May I leave to make final preparations, milord?"

"Of course. You can take off when you're ready. Drop a white marker where you land so we know where you are."

Wynter nodded and left.

Karne turned to Orkonan. "Tane, I'm leaving you in charge here. Draft a statement to that effect and I'll sign it. No telling what Old Party men might try once it's learned that I'm away."

"Yan, Dennen, thank the earl for his offer and decline it for me, please. I'll be too busy to talk to outsiders myself for awhile. You two are welcome to join us if you want."

Dennen shook his head. "We can't wear your colors and the earl doesn't want ours shown, not at Breven."

Karne shrugged and stood. "That's the way it is, then. No hard feelings. You've fought with us elsewhere. See you when we get back." He headed for the iron stair to his quarters.

The two Willems looked stung by the abrupt dismissal, but stood and left the room.

Nik followed Karne up the stair. "How many men are you going to send down after Richard, Karne?"

"A troop to start, then as many as it takes to get Kit back or to convince me there's no chance of her surviving any more attacks."

"What then? What will we do then?"

"Shut up, Nik! I know you're worried and afraid for Kit. So am I, so SHUT UP!"

Karne moved through his quarters like a whirlwind, scooping up this or that, jamming one thing into a pocket, clipping another to his belt. The last thing he picked up was a long rectangular object too big for a pocket. He started down the stair again, his equipment now banging and jingling.

"What's that?" Nik asked.

"A trap controller. Or it's supposed to be." Karne skipped the last step entirely and hit the library floor at a lope. He explained no further until he and Nik were in the lead flier headed west. "Richard's using one of the Old Ones' tunnels, but there are others, deeper, going to the ruins and other places. Weisman's found a map, partial, of course, but a map of some of them. Egil left the controller with me when he went home.

He said it would prevent the Old Ones' traps from operating."
Karne paused a moment, deep in thought. "If there's no other
way to get to Kit, we can come through the tunnels from the
outside. Maybe."

Nik thought about that in silence for a time. When he finally
spoke, it was with unusual hesitation. "With all due respect
to Egil, Karne, what proof do you have that this 'controller'
works?"

"Egil's word."

"And that's enough to risk your life on?" Nik sounded
incredulous.

Karne nodded. "It has to be. Our only chance is surprise.
If Richard's warned, he can defend himself under Breven forever. The tunnels would then be Kit's only hope. Egil said
he'd never had to use it but he was sure it worked. Wherever
he got it, he didn't take it from Richard when he captured him.
If Richard had such things, he wouldn't have had to sacrifice
soldiers to the traps outside Breven."

"If he had such devices, do you think he'd let anyone else
know?" Nik's voice was sharp. "He wouldn't've used it to
save his soldiers, because they'd tell other soldiers and soon
the whole planet would know there was a safe way into the
ruins."

Karne had his own doubts about the efficacy of the controller,
but he was not going to share those with anyone.

CHAPTER 14

I offered the soldiers no resistance. There was no point. My only escape was to die, and I didn't think Richard would let that happen, no matter how I tried. I wondered how they planned to get me into a men's Retreat House, but I didn't have to wonder long. They tugged a deacon's robe over my head and down over my clothes, then pulled up its hood.

"Say nothing if you wish to keep your tongue," the squad leader in charge said.

I remembered Miri and believed him. My tongue was not a part of my body Richard was interested in. As far as he was concerned, I didn't need it. Not for his purposes, anyway. The soldiers marched me to the Retreat House, across the courtyard, and immediately up to the second level. This was a building above the surface, where men lived year round. The Retreat Houses had always been a wonder to me because of this. I had read about the extremely thick walls and the huge insulated shutters that filled the window openings for the winter, but I hadn't believed those could be enough. They would not have been enough at McNeece's hunting lodge, which was why the lodge had deep underground levels. Now I had a chance to examine it, to see how such a place could be survivable. I let myself dwell on these details because they diverted my mind, however briefly, from what was going to happen to me very soon.

The Harlan squad leader pressed me unceremoniously onto a bench in the hallway, then went through an elaborately carved door into what I suspected was the abbot's office or apartment. I was not going to get to see the Retreat House, then, only this hallway. Muffled sounds of anger, argument, pleading, demanding, came through the door, but not the words that would have allowed me to make sense of what was going on. The bench was hard, it had been a very long time since I'd seen a Sanitary, and longer since I'd eaten. I dared not ask for relief of any kind. Not if I valued my tongue.

After what seemed like a very long time, the squad leader came out and motioned his squad in the direction of the stairway. A stocky prefet asked permission to speak, and, when the squad leader granted it, whispered something in his ear. The squad leader looked over at me speculatively.

"You need to clean up before we present you to the duke," he snapped. "One moment." He spun and rapped sharply on the abbot's door.

I shot the prefet a look of gratitude.

"I have a sister," he murmured, then looked quickly away to study spider webs at the joint of wall and ceiling.

After a considerable amount of arguing and shouting behind the abbot's door, the door opened and the abbot beckoned me in with a reluctant hand. "Not a word," he snarled. "Not one word. You never came to Breven." But he pointed toward a small door in a corner of his lavish room.

I hurried through it. The facilities were more elaborate and more expensive than anything we had at Ontar. I hadn't realized leaders of Retreat Houses lived in such luxury. Then I thought of Aunt Alba and realized they didn't. Right then it didn't matter. I had relief after hours and hours and then time to clean the dirt of weeks with the Gypsies from me, or at least from the visible parts of me. If I had to go to Richard, I didn't have to go to him dirty.

I took as much time as I dared. I didn't want to meet Richard of Harlan, much though I'd heard of his charm. Charm wasn't necessary with a captive enemy. Finally, the squad leader unceremoniously opened the Sanitary door and dragged me out.

"Not a word," he reminded me as he dragged me across the abbot's carpet and out his door.

There was a lift beyond the stairs we had come up. We used the lift. A lift was quick and out of sight, which was for the soldiers' benefit, because there weren't supposed to be any soldiers in any Retreat House, ever. I wondered where all the legitimate guests were and decided they were probably at night-meal. I wondered how many of them knew Richard had soldiers with him.

The lift went down. That surprised me. I would've expected Richard to have an upper-floor room with a magnificent view. The lift door opened into a dimly lighted hallway. At the far right end, a Harlan soldier stood, outlined in light coming from a side hallway. He raised his arm when he saw the soldiers with me.

"Stay here," the squad leader ordered. "I'll see what his lordship's orders are."

The squad leader trotted down the hall and disappeared around the corner. I drew my arms inside the body of the habit, a relatively easy thing to do without much noticeable movement, thanks to the habit's deep sleeve openings. I clenched my hands together there, out of sight, to conceal how frightened I was. I knew I was pale, for my cheeks felt cold, but *that* the dim lighting probably concealed. Nothing would have concealed the twisting of my hands if they had been in plain sight.

The squad leader reappeared, and Richard with him. Richard moved ahead, coming toward me with catlike silence and grace. He made a sweeping bow, far deeper than was necessary or even polite. Perhaps he exaggerated it to be sure I saw it from the shelter of the hood.

"Lady Kathryn," he said. "I'm so pleased to see you." He knelt in a beautiful, fluid movement and lifted my hand to his forehead in the ritual gesture of deep respect. He had made the same gesture toward my mother at the Council meeting during which he had killed her. He looked at me as he rose and I knew he remembered, too. He not only remembered, but had deliberately stirred up that memory to remind me he had already killed one woman.

He looked over my shoulder. "Where's Ennis?"

I wanted to throw back the hood and look directly at him, but I dared not. His men had hooded me. I must stay that way until he said otherwise. "He—he left me alone some days ago, milord."

He frowned. "And your beautiful daughter?"

"Gone, too, milord. I know not where. A husband has that right, milord." I needed no skill at acting to make my voice full of tears. It was.

Richard glanced at the squad leader.

"It's true, milord. Odonnel tried very skillfully to find out where the betrayer had gone. If the lady had known, she would have told him. She told him nothing."

Richard pushed back my hood. "Any scars," he asked the squad leader as he examined my face. He beckoned the man with the light to come closer.

The squad leader bowed. "He knows your tastes, milord. The duress was great, but he left visible only bruises and these and the other injuries have had more than a month to heal."

"Good." Richard tipped my face up. "I don't deal in damaged goods," he told me, his eyes as cold as a snake's. "If Garren had damaged you, I'm afraid I would've given up my original plan for revenge against your House and given you to my men instead. For as long as you lasted."

I remembered the Gypsy women and shivered. Richard saw the movement and smiled a slow, cold smile. "I see you understand." He released my chin and the character of his face changed in an instant from cruel political plotter to the charming singer of ballads, the man who was the dream of many women. He put his arm around me. "I'd hoped, four years ago, that our Houses would cease to be at war, my lady." His voice was smooth and seductive. His hand slid around my waist. He bent to whisper in my ear. "There's another way the feud can be ended." He pulled me full against his body and kissed me in a way that left no doubt of his meaning. A male child would end the feud by his mere existence.

The soldiers around us snorted or covered their mouths with their hands to smother their chuckles. My stomach heaved and I wanted to throw up. Richard straightened and looked down at me. We were in the light from the side hall now and his face showed no arousal at all. It had all been technique and performance. I had no doubt that this performance, and ribald speculation about what more he would do once we were alone, would amuse all the members of his garrison tonight, and the rest of Harlan as soon as some of these soldiers went on leave.

His face darkened and he bent to kiss me again, even more indecently, one hand grinding my hips against his, the other fumbling with my buttons. I thanked the Guardians I had worn a dress that buttoned down the back. Then he switched character again instantly. His hands fell away from me and he turned to the squad leader. ''Take her to the rooms prepared. I plan to begin my child's begetting at the opening hour of Council in the morning.''

In the morning. How like him that timing was. Massacre on my wedding day. Forced wedding on my birthday. Now this. Perhaps Richard would even tell Karne what he was going to do. In the morning he would tell him, when Karne was too far away and too bound by his duty to Halarek to prevent it. Karne *had* to be at Council.

Two soldiers came forward and each took an arm. In a few moments I saw why. They were going to take me into a tunnel of the Old Ones, a tunnel clearly marked ''Warning! Stay Out.'' Two more soldiers guarded its entrance. For a second I considered struggling, then decided dying in a trap laid by the Old Ones was better than dying in a trap laid by Richard.

I need not have feared the Old Ones' traps. Harlan soldiers had sprung them already and died doing it. We passed one sprung trap, a deep hole that now had a board over it, and then another, a slab that had fallen from the ceiling onto its victim. There was also a rockfall, which had had to be cleared away enough for us to pass, a pit with sharp stakes in its bottom, and a trap that apparently loosed an energy bolt of some sort, for the remains on the floor had a huge charred hole in its chest. Richard had left the men where the traps had killed them. He had not even had the decency to bring out what was left of them for burial.

The soldiers turned into a dark place and set a belt Torch into a wall bracket. The light illuminated a small room furnished with heavy, ornate furniture. The door had my full name painted on it, but the room had been recently lived in, for there was a faint trace of perfume and hair oil in the air, and a brush with long dark hairs in it still lay on the small table beside the bed. The Old Ones had made the room, because it was not newly cut from the rock, though I had no doubt it could have been, had Richard wished it. I wondered what use it had been to the Old Ones.

"Your room, my lady," one of the soldiers said.

"Sleep well and pleasant dreams," the other said with a leer.

They left the room, shutting the door behind them. They didn't trouble to lock the door. Why should they? There were only two places to run. Toward Richard, where a guard stood watch at the mouth of the tunnel, or deeper into the territory of the Old Ones. Five sprung traps told what happened to anyone who tried *that*.

The first thing I did once I was alone was look for a weapon, any sort of weapon. A knife, a fork, a bottle or glass that could be broken, a piece of furniture that could be used as a club— there was nothing except, perhaps, the furniture, and I quickly discovered that that was too heavy for me to lift, let alone swing hard enough to break it. Perhaps death in a tunnel *was* my choice.

I lifted the Torch from its bracket on the wall and searched more carefully. The only possible weapon was the bar on the inside of the door, and there was nothing in the room I could use to pry out the staples that held it in place. I sat on the bed. The long-feared fate had come. I was to be Richard's whore.

There comes a time when fear no longer makes the heart pound and the breath come faster. I had reached that point. There was nothing I could do to save myself except to run down the tunnel and die. I didn't want to die yet. Ennis and I had produced a child. I cared for and respected Ennis. I loved the child. It might be difficult for Ennis, but, given the opportunity, he would love a child of Richard's begetting if it were also mine. I knew just as surely that Richard would have Ennis killed at the earliest opportunity. I wished I had been able to love Ennis as he deserved.

Would coupling with Richard be so much different from the first few times with Ennis? Much as I tried to convince myself otherwise, I knew it would. It couldn't help but be. Ennis had been obeying orders for the genetic good of his House. Richard was acting out his own desire for vengeance on Halarek. Ennis had been slow and gentle. Richard would not be. Coupling with Richard would be terrible. He'd make sure it was. I could choose death without dishonor in the traps, or dishonor without death in Richard's room. It was a much harder decision than it sounds like to people who've never had to make such a choice. Such decisions *are* easy, if you don't have to face the consequences of choosing.

I may have sat long in that fog of indecision. Noises from the end of the tunnel roused me from despair. I sat straighter and listened carefully. Men shouted. I ran to the door and looked out. Beamers hissed at the end of the tunnel. I heard a scream. A few moments later, a soldier in Halarek blue appeared out of the darkness beyond my door. I stared at him in disbelief. Soldiers, our soldiers, here!

"Here, Lord Nik!" he called over his shoulder. "Are you all right?" he asked me with concern.

I knew what he meant. I nodded, still speechless with shock.

Nik and six more soldiers sprinted down the tunnel toward us, four in Halarek blue, one in von Schuss brown, one in plain clothes. Bodies in green and brown and blue wrestled and fired and dodged or ducked or crumpled to the floor at the mouth of the tunnel.

"Spread out!" Nik said.

The man in plain clothes immediately crossed the hall, leaned against the wall to steady himself, and fired at green uniforms just then running into the tunnel.

"May as well," said the soldier in brown, moving across the tunnel. "If we back into the Lady Kathryn's room, our backs are protected but the beamers'll bake us. If we don't, we fry right here."

The other three arranged themselves across the passage. The Harlan soldiers, six of them, gave a shout as they saw their opponents and rushed forward. Our defenders fired. There was the biting smell of ozone. One of the Harlan men fell. The rest fired back. One of the Halarek Specials screamed and sagged against the tunnel wall, his uniform sleeve charred and smoking.

"Stand behind me." Nik grabbed my wrist and tugged.

I snatched my hand back. "Don't be a fool!" I know I snarled, but I'd never been shot at before and I was very frightened. "We need another fighter, not a hider."

I scrambled across the tunnel, keeping my body low, and slid the dead Special's stunner from his hand and his knife from his belt. A beamer bolt seared the back of my neck. I dropped to the cold stone and slapped at my burning hair.

"Kit!"

"Don't worry."

The man in plain clothes gasped and folded up on himself. His beamer fell to the stone with a clatter. "Run, lord," the man gasped. "Too many reinforcements. Take the lady and run!"

The soldiers in green were only four or five meters away. It's hard to miss at that distance, for either side. Nik looked at the soldiers, then glanced over his shoulder at the darkness of the tunnel.

"There's no other way, lord," the soldier who had come to my door said. One of his arms dangled at his side, the hand burned past using. "We can hold them off a few minutes more, no longer."

"The controller," Nik muttered. His hand went to his belt.

I remembered Egil's controller. No one had ever used it. A beamer bolt hissed past my ear. Nik flinched and swore. An untested device, the controller was, and for one of the most dangerous areas on Starker IV. More soldiers in green piled through the tunnel mouth. Five against so many—

"Take the controller." Nik thrust it into my hand. "I need both hands. You keep that center button pressed until we get away or they catch us or it fails." He tore a strip of fabric from the hem of his tunic, tied it over the face of his belt Torch, and gripped the Torch in his left hand. He shot the beam of light down the tunnel. It was dim, so we wouldn't make good targets. "Come!" he snapped. He whirled away from the battle and ran down the tunnel.

I pressed the button and held it, then followed. I didn't have to ask him how I'd know if it failed. I glanced over my shoulder. The two lines of men had met. We didn't have long. Either we got quickly out of sight or Harlan soldiers would catch us. Our men couldn't hold out long against superior numbers.

Maybe one of the traps would catch us. I stumbled down that darkened tunnel and squashed thoughts of what it would feel like to die in a trap.

The air was cold. I was tiring faster than I would ever have believed. Someone behind shouted to us, "Halarek lives! Run!" The cry was like a boost of energy. I ran. The tunnel narrowed. Torchlight now followed us from behind. I prayed for a trap to stop the soldiers. The air was thick with the dust we stirred up, and musty. The dust muffled the sounds of our running feet. The sounds of battle behind us ended. The dust caught in my throat and made me cough. I tried not to think about our defenders. I tried only to keep my feet from stumbling and my finger from slipping from the controller button. What if a trap had already been sprung ahead of us, a pit trap, for instance? Boots pounded closer behind us. Nik gripped the Torch handle between his teeth and dialed his stunner to "kill." I glanced over my shoulder. Three men in green followed close behind. I stumbled and my finger slid partway off the button. For a moment, my heart stopped, but no trap opened under our feet or fell onto us from above. I heard the Harlan men's harsh panting. The skin across my back tightened as if their fingers were already clawing at it. I knew they weren't firing because they intended to take me back to Richard.

"Harlan," I managed to gasp. "Close."

Nik skidded to a stop and turned to face the way we'd come. "Take the cover off the Torch when I tell you. Ready?"

I gripped an edge of the cloth. "Yes."

"Now!" Nik ordered.

I jerked the cloth off. Nik flashed the Torch's brightest light at our pursuers. The three men in Harlan green yelled and held their arms over their eyes.

"They'll only be blind for seconds, Nik."

Nik fired four times down the tunnel, then turned and ran. There's no way to know if a stunner hits its target without time and good light, and the light was only good at our end. I struggled to keep up with him.

A very bright light came on behind us, and then I heard the sound of light, swift feet. We had gained a little distance and the Harlan men weren't counting on being within range of whatever protected us anymore. They were sending a swift, light man through the traps, a man so light or so fast that he might get through without setting them off. It had been tried before. I could think of only once that the man had not died anyway, and that man had been lucky enough to be in a tunnel under a very large building, so he could be rescued by a shaft drilled into the tunnel from a level above it. This man had to be very brave, because there was nothing above us now but rock.

A beamer bolt sizzled between us. The runner hadn't been sent to catch us, but to kill! I stumbled. Another bolt zipped past. Nik gasped. The man was going to kill Nik!

"Release the button," Nik ordered. "Now!"

I obeyed without question. Nik shoved me to the floor. A beam seared over us right where Nik had been.

"That one was right on target," Nik whispered in my ear.

There was a creak, then an ominous shifting sound, then a slab of rock dropped from the roof of the tunnel onto the floor about a meter behind us. It cracked when it hit and sprayed us with daggers of rock. An instant later another slab of rock slammed into the floor ahead of us. We clung together while the dust of centuries swirled around us, choking us and making our eyelids grate against our eyes. The last chunk of rock clinked across the big slab and hit the dusty floor with a dull sound. The dust settled slowly. The small area remaining was dark except for a reddish glow at the edge of the slab behind us. I directed our Torch beam toward it. A bend of elbow stuck out from under pieces broken from the slab. The glow was from a Torch or beamer in his hand. That was how close the Harlan soldier had been. He had almost made it through. *He* was dead. *We* were trapped, which might mean the same thing.

CHAPTER 15

The stars were coming out when Karne and his force arrived over Breven. The Retreat House had no lights for night landings, because pilgrims and retreat makers did not arrive at night. The fliers overhead, then, would not be recognized. They might not even be noticed. Karne circled once around the dark square of the Retreat, squatting in the middle of its compound and gardens. Here and there a window still sent out a band of yellow light. Karne turned toward Loch and flew as low over the forest as he dared, hoping even in the growing darkness to see the white marker Wynter's men were to have set out.

"There. To the left." Karne spoke softly into the inter-flier com unit.

A square of white cloth lay in a large clearing. As Karne flew over, someone illuminated the cloth for a moment with Torchlight. Karne murmured a brief prayer for safety, then nosed his flier toward the landing area. It landed with a bound. The moment the flier slowed to a crawl, men darted from the darkness under nearby trees, threaded hooks through the flier's tie-down loops, and hauled it into the forest, hiding it and clearing the landing spot for the next flier at the same time. It was very dangerous, landing in such a small area in the dark, both for the men in the fliers and the men on the ground, but it could not be helped.

The Guardians were with them. No one at Breven raised an alarm. Eight days later, after dark, a man in a deacon's habit came into Karne's tent. His breath sobbed in and out in great gasps.

"Gypsies, Lord Karne. Sunset. Killed Harlan soldiers. Gone."

"Sunset?" Criticism was sharply plain in Karne's voice.

"My—my lord." The man collapsed into a sitting position. His head drooped far forward. Karne had to crouch to hear the rest of the message.

"My lord, couldn't come by flitter. Be seen." He stopped, struggling for air.

Karne held his impatience in check, but only with considerable effort. Kit, Kit, Kit, one side of him kept saying. The man's clearly exhausted, another side said. Give him time.

"I ran the whole way, milord. Harlan men brought a new deacon in. Hours after the Gypsies."

Karne nodded. "I understand now. In that case you've done very good work. Get yourself some nightmeal and some rest."

Nik turned to Karne before the man left the tent and his voice was hard. "Get what men you can and let's go!"

One look at Nik told Karne that if he did not go, Nik would go anyway, with whatever men he could collect. Karne slipped his Torch from its belt clip, flashed its light on his face once and cried, "Halarek lives! Specials to me!"

Nik shouted. "Von Schuss! To me, to me!"

Men grabbed their equipment from wherever it lay and ran toward their fliers. Karne knew that the Specials, at least, could be counted on to have the tools needed.

"Lady Kathryn's been taken in already!" Karne shouted.

The men of Halarek growled, a noise that quickly turned into a roar. Knowing Nik wanted to lead the attack, Karne had spoken quickly to be sure the men followed *him*. Nik was far too caught up in his own feelings about Kit to be a good leader. Inside the Retreat, Wynter would be in command of both forces, as agreed. Nik sprinted off to a flitter as soon as he saw the first of his called men pick up their weapons. The rest of the von Schuss men followed his example. Karne cursed softly.

Karne found Wynter among the crowd, motioned him to go, and hoped they would be in time to prevent Richard from injuring Kit or to prevent Nik from injuring Richard. Within the laws of feud, Nik had no right to interfere at all. To injure Richard or, worse, kill him without legal "provocation" would be enough to drag House von Schuss into feud with Harlan.

There was a more important reason than that for keeping Richard alive: Richard would rather die the worst death imaginable than live a prisoner in Breven, so continuing life for Richard Harlan was Karne's best revenge. Egil had learned that during his pursuit of Richard. The duke-designate had taunted and insulted Egil, trying to provoke Egil into killing him so he would not have to go back to Breven.

Then the time for worrying about what Nik was doing was gone. They were over Lake St. Paul and then over Breven. Minutes later, the fliers landed and the men were at the wall. The Retreat's main gates were open. Karne saw Wynter sprint through the gates, followed by the soldiers who had taken off when he did. When Karne himself reached the courtyard moments later, everyone was still there, waiting for him, including Nik and his men. Karne felt a moment's relief, for he had feared Nik's reckless eagerness might have drawn them after him.

Wynter jerked his head toward the stair. "I'll send half the men—the first squad each of von Schuss and Halarek—upstairs, milord. You and Lord Nicholas go below with the rest. The work there requires the rank of lords of the Families. You take care of the Heir in Harlan. I'll mind the battle." He paused for objections from Karne or Nik, and when there were none, he turned to the men. He pointed out the soldiers who were to go upstairs and gave them their orders.

"Go quietly. Courteously awaken the abbot and keep him strictly confined to his quarters. Let him talk to or signal no one."

Karne saw several of the soldiers near him smile. He, too, could imagine the abbot's discomfiture at being awakened, getting worse when he learned he had been awakened because his crimes had been found out.

Wynter continued. "The rest, follow me to Richard Harlan's secret quarters two levels down. Have your weapons out and at ready."

Karne turned. Nik was already gone, and a squad of von Schuss men with him. Karne and Wynter followed. The rest of the soldiers came quickly and quietly after, as quietly as men can with belts full of equipment that jangles and rattles and with only one hand to stifle the noise. Karne halted with raised hand at the bottom of the last stair. Nik had had the sense to stop under the steps and wait until the others came. When the rattles and jangles caused by stopping had died away, Karne looked out into the hall. Two guards stood as before at the entrance to the corridor leading to Richard's suite.

"My lord," Wynter said.

Karne turned to the men on the stair and spoke in a low but carrying voice. "Remember, the duke-designate is *not* to be harmed. My vengeance is best served if he lives in solitary confinement for seven more years. *Much* better served."

Karne looked at the nearest Specials and jerked his head toward the guards.

"Get them."

The men removed their equipment belts, but took their knives. They flattened themselves against the same wall that the guards stood against and slipped silently toward them. Halfway there, they stopped to listen. Karne found himself willing the guards not to look toward the stairwell. The Specials in the hall slid into motion again. Suddenly they lunged. Each grabbed a guard and slit his throat without a sound, then they flattened themselves against the sides of the entryway and beckoned the men in the stairwell toward them.

"Good," Wynter said, almost to himself. "Good work!" In a more normal voice he said, "You and Lord Nicholas take care of Lord Richard. That's for men of the Nine. I'll take care of the others."

Karne nodded.

"I'll get Kit," Nik said in Karne's ear. "If she and Richard aren't already—" He choked on the idea, then went on. "Her room's down the tunnel. Give me the trap controller."

Karne's face must have shown his surprise, even in the twilight illumination of that lower hall, because Nik snapped,

"What if she's in that room with her name on the door? Give us a chance if we get trapped down there, Karne!"

Karne wanted to argue, but there wasn't time. Any moment someone might come out of Richard's suite or down the stairs. He unclipped the controller and handed it over.

Wynter looked at the men in the stairwell behind him. "Silence your equipment as best you can," he told them. "Surprise is the best offense." He then led the soldiers out into the hall.

They reached the branch corridor without discovery. Beyond that there would be no chance of secrecy. Two Specials slipped around the corner ahead of the other men and sprinted to the doorway guarded by deacons. The two young men were watching what was going on in the suite through the open door, so the Specials captured them without as much as a squawk from either man. The moment the deacons had been silenced, Karne and Nik sprang into the main room. Richard, playing chess with one of his troopleaders, leaped to his feet, knocking over the small table and spilling the chess pieces all over the floor. His face went white, then red. In the fraction of a second it took for Richard to realize what had happened and to shout for his men, Karne saw Kit was not there. Halarek and von Schuss men poured into the room.

"She's not here!" Karne shouted to Nik, who was wrestling near the door with a brawny man in green.

Karne turned and began fighting his way toward Richard. Richard's bodyguard appeared from the adjoining room and more poured into the suite from the hall. Men fought with knives, stunners, or any of hundreds of weaponless methods, but not beamers. No one used beamers in close combat: They created intense heat in close quarters and did terrible damage to friend as well as foe. The flood of enemies washed over Karne and he had no more time to look for Kit.

Karne dodged a knife thrust, parried another, then twisted away from a kick coming at him from the side. He jammed his stunner under his belt, grabbed the foot of the kicker, and jerked it before the man could get his balance. The man fell under the feet of the fighters with a sharp cry. A burly Harlan prefet charged through the door at the head of a squad. He slammed a heavy fist into Karne's ribs. Karne staggered backward. A von Schuss prefet lunged across him before he caught his balance and slipped his knife into the burly soldier. All around men shouted or grunted with effort or groaned in pain. A young soldier in green aimed a stunner at the von Schuss man, but one of Halarek's Specials shoved a Harlan guard into the path of the beam. The guard fell silently. Karne did not pause to see if the man were dead or merely unconscious, but leaped over the body to protect the von Schuss man from a killing hand-blow. He felt a sudden weakness on his left side and knew he had caught the edge of a stunner beam. The man next to him fell over and flopped onto his back, eyes staring at the ceiling. Karne spun, knocked the Harlan soldier's stunner upward, then tried to twist it out of the man's hand. The soldier wrapped one leg around Karne's and strained to trip him. They swayed back and forth. Karne fought for balance. A pair of men, pummeling each other on the floor, rolled into their legs and Karne and the Harlan soldier fell, tangled with each other. As he went down, Karne saw Nik slip quickly into the adjoining room and slip back out almost as quickly. No Kit.

In that momentary distraction, Karne's grip loosened a fraction. The Harlan soldier twisted Karne's hand until the stunner pointed at his chest. Even if the weapon were set only to stun, at that range and so near his heart, it would kill. The world for Karne narrowed to the tiny space where he fought the young soldier for control of the stunner. The soldier slowly squeezed Karne's finger tighter on the trigger. A man in brown and gold tripped on the Harlan soldier's elbow and tumbled onto them, jamming the stunner into Karne's belly and temporarily knocking the wind out of all of them.

Karne recovered first. He rolled on top of the Harlan soldier, who fired. The stunner beam shot along Karne's leg, numbing his right knee and toes and bringing down three or four fighters in its path by taking the feeling from their legs. Karne, his weight holding the soldier somewhat still, slid his knife between the soldier's ribs, then gave the little twist Wynter had said always resulted in fatal damage.

Karne attempted to climb to his feet. His right knee and foot would not support him and he fell sideways onto men already fallen. A beamer bolt sizzled over him. It burned through a von Schuss man and charred a large circle on the wall behind him. Karne lay where he was and looked for the source of the beam. Richard stood against the outer door, steadying a beamer and swinging his head from side to side. Karne knew Richard was trying to find him again.

He sees his soft life ending and he intends to end me first, Karne thought. Not if I can help it.

Karne crawled slowly toward Richard, flattening himself against the floor or rolling out of the way as necessary. If he could get within a few feet of Richard without being seen, he had a chance to take the beamer. Richard would not look for him on the floor. Karne's shin tingled. Perhaps he would be able to use the leg again soon. It was waking up. If Richard did not find Karne, he would probably continue to roast people, until the room became too warm for his comfort. Karne could almost feel the beamer scars that covered his back pulling tight again, scars from an assassination attempt his first year home. Richard had to be stopped. No one should have to go through such pain.

Karne rose to his hands and knees. His right knee supported him, though it was wobbly. He had worked his way to within two meters of Richard and was slightly behind him. Honor required he tell his opponent he was there. The duke-designate in Harlan was not a common soldier, after all. Common sense and self-preservation told Karne to be well within striking distance before he said anything. He stopped a little more than an arm's reach away, crouched to spring, and took a deep, steadying breath.

A second. The knee must hold for a second. ''Richard Harlan, I'm here!'' he called out and lunged for Richard's gun hand.

Richard spun, spraying everyone in his path with fire. Karne ducked under the hand, came up swiftly, grabbed the gun from the side and bent Richard's hand sharply in toward his forearm. Richard's hand opened involuntarily even as he spun to grab Karne with his free hand. The groans of the burned men spurred Karne on. As Richard whirled to grab him, Karne yielded, moving backward as Richard spun forward, using Richard's arm as a turning point. Richard's own momentum spun him face-first into the wall behind them. Karne heard a wet crunch with savage satisfaction. Small repayment for the terror Kit had gone through. He hoped the nose was broken severely enough that it would never again have the long, thin beauty so

admired in the Harlan line. Karne wrenched Richard's other
hand behind him and bound the two together with a thin strong
line from his equipment belt.

For the first time since the battle began, Karne heard his
own breath. It rasped in and out. His lungs struggled to get
enough air. Blood ran warm down one leg. A burn on the back
of his left hand began to shoot fire up his arm. He had not
known he had wounds. He leaned against the wall for support
and looked around him. Only a few men in green remained on
their feet, far fewer than wore blue or brown. They had won,
von Schuss and Halarek. He looked again at the room. Many
of the motionless bodies on the floor also wore blue or brown.
At what cost had they won? This was a question he always
asked himself, though he knew it made him a weaker commander.

Karne shouted to the men still fighting. "Stop! It's over.
The Harlan is bound."

The fighting stopped almost at once. The men stood panting,
waiting for instructions. Karne beckoned to four Specials.

"Take the duke-designate to a vacant retreat room, have
food sent up, then lock him in and guard the door with your
lives. Council must know of his way of living here and of the
battle we've fought. What time is it?"

"Two hours of 15 Aden, milord," one of the Specials said.

"By the Guardians!" Karne looked around. "Where's Lord
Nicholas?"

"He learned Lady Kathryn had been confined down that
tunnel, my lord." The Special pointed to the place of the Old
Ones. "He said he'd get her and bring her back."

"He took six soldiers with him, milord," said another of
the Specials.

Karne hesitated only a moment. The flight to Council ground
from Breven was eight hours in good weather. If he left immediately, he would arrive at Council at its opening, or nearly.

"Any pursuit?" he asked the Specials.

They shrugged. "We had our hands full just then, milord."

Karne wished he knew where on the agenda his proposal to
confine Richard and depose the abbot was. He wished he had
gone for Kit himself. He wished—

He had to leave. Nik was competent, even if too tied up in

emotions. He had probably taken all the men that could be spared from the main battle. He could rescue Kit without Karne's assistance. Richard would be securely confined, at least until Council adjourned. Ennis would witness to Richard's violations of Council sentence and to his plan to violate the Nine's laws of inheritance. Ennis would need a strong guard, but Van would already have arranged that.

I have to trust people to do their duty. I have to trust my officers to carry out my orders. I have to find faith that Nik and Kit will be all right.

Karne looked at the nearest captain of Specials. ''Take the duke-designate away,'' he told the man. ''Confine the rest of the Harlans as you think best. If you have questions or need authorizations for anything, ask General Wynter. I must get to Council.''

Karne limped down the hall and up the stairs. He knew he should at least take time to have the Specials' medic look at his burn, but he did not have the time.

When he reached the courtyard, Karne stood a moment, getting his breath and easing his leg, then climbed into his flitter and took off for Council. Guilt gnawed at him. The people who meant most to him had disappeared down a tunnel of the Old Ones and he was leaving them there. He was deserting them. He kept telling himself he had left both Breven and Kit's rescue in competent hands, but the guilt would not go away.

With effort Karne wrenched his thoughts from Breven to the meeting ahead and how he must handle it. His body he could not keep under such rigid control. His hands sweated enough to slip on the control wheel. His teeth clenched and unclenched until his jaws ached. He had to win the battle at Council, too.

CHAPTER 16

Karne landed at Council without incident. When he swung his legs out of the door onto the flitter's wing, he discovered how stiff they were. Again the idea of having the wounds seen to crossed his mind, but here, at Council, the visible effects of the battle under Breven had political value just as they were.

Inside the Council building, men in House and freecity colors moved against a background of blue mosaics and political chatter. The smells of klag, wet wool, leather polish, and perfumes filled the air. The clamor of voices was enough to make ears ring. Karne hobbled toward the Council chamber's main doors.

A centen in McNeece colors caught Karne's eye, then motioned with his head for Karne to join him in the lift to the lower levels. Karne followed, but with one hand on his stunner. Anyone could steal or buy House or freecity colors. He had done it himself. Once inside the lift with the door closed, the centen showed Karne a baby's tie-on slipper.

"The owner is well," the centen said. His flushed face and the ways his eyes slid away from direct contact with Karne's showed the man felt most uncomfortable with such an unwarrior-like object as identification. "The owner's master is safe below and will come upstairs as arranged, if needed."

Because Ennis, and Narra, were far safer if almost no one knew where they were, Van and Karne had agreed Ennis would be kept out of sight unless needed. Van, in the person of his man, obviously thought a courtesy visit was in order. And this must be a McNeece man: No respectable spy would think of such a feminine item as a recognition sign.

Ennis waited in one of the luxurious rooms reserved for "guests" of Council. His face was pale and rigid with tension. Karne had spent many frightening hours under arrest in such a room himself, an arrest he only later learned was for his own protection. He greeted Ennis with words of appreciation for what he had been willing to do for Kit and Narra. Such appreciation was not a usual thing between men of the Gharr, but Karne believed the words were necessary, though they caught in his throat. He hoped Van and his guard did not think less of him for it. Karne moved on quickly, giving Ennis a summary of the battle at Breven, including Kit's disappearance down a tunnel of the Old Ones, then excused himself.

He hurried back to chamber level. From then until the session opened, Karne hovered outside the Council chamber's big central doors, checking off allies in his mind as they entered the chamber. The deep blue mosaics, which were supposed to have a calming effect, did not work on him this day. Too much was riding on Council's vote. Karne ran over in his head again and again the speech he had planned. He hoped Ennis, tightly guarded as he was, would still have the courage to leave that security and face Council if necessary. He hoped even more strongly that Ennis would live to finish his testimony. One murder had been committed in Council. Another could be.

A heavy arm fell across his shoulders. Karne looked over and smiled thinly at the plump, balding man in brown and gold beside him.

"Peace be on your House, Baron."

Having successfully gained Karne's attention, the baron withdrew his arm. "And on yours, Karne. How goes it?"

"Guardians! I wish I knew. Too many Freemen still see Richard's violations of the law as "Family business" or a matter for The Way and none of their concern. Without a majority of Freemen voting with us, we lose."

The baron looked grim, patted Karne on the shoulder, then headed for the chamber's doors. Four men in Council-red uniforms blew the assembly signal on trumpets, and the men remaining in the hall began filing into the chamber. Karne made one last contact with each of the weakest links in his coalition; reminded Gareth, who was waiting by the doors, to bring Ennis upstairs when sent for; then went into the chamber and down the aisle between the Justin and Halarek back benches to his place at the prep table of his House. Tane Orkonan sat ready, his writing materials arranged neatly in front of him. Slowly the other lords of the Nine took places at their tables along with their secretaries, administrators, and Heirs. The brothers, sons, uncles, and cousins of each House filled the rows of benches behind each lord's table.

In the other half of the room, the Freemen and the men of the minor Houses filled their sections. Karne reminded himself that victory lay with the Freemen and minor Houses, not the Nine. Thanks be to the Guardians, not with the Nine!

Trumpets blew again and the chairman marched down an aisle to the polished desk in the center of the chamber.

"Chairman Gashen of the freecity of Neeran," one of the men in red announced.

Chairman Gashen looked around the room to see if most of the ranks of benches were full. He nodded and sat down at his desk. "The summer Council of Starker IV is now in session. Will the clerk please read the agenda?"

The agenda included a dispute between House McNeece and House Kath over a parcel of grazing land, a new proposal in Starker IV's trade agreement with the Gild, recognition of new Heirs in seven minor Houses, a petition to station Council soldiers at Breven to see that Council sentence was actually carried out, and a petition from the merchants' association of Londor to set up a new trade in wool cloth there. Members from the freecity of York muttered over this notice. Chairman Gashen looked severely in their direction and they silenced themselves.

Near the end, Karne thought. The matter of the abbot and of Richard's sentence comes near the end. Well, perhaps the members will have the fight worn out of them by then and they'll be more willing to listen to reason.

Debate on the various issues dragged on and on. Karne found himself fidgeting, impatient as a child in church. When the chairman finally announced "the proposal having to do with Breven," Karne found his palms sweating again. He was confronting not only Harlan supporters here, but traditionalists among followers of The Way, who would not support any action by Council against an abbot.

He stood and ran over his speech again in one part of his mind while another part checked the crowd to be sure no supporters had left in boredom or aggravation. They had all stayed. When the chairman had again rapped the Council to order, Karne stepped into the open area ahead of the chairman's desk.

"Mr. Chairman," he said, turning and bowing to Gashen. "Lords and Freemen." He looked at every sector of the circle of Council. "My—our—proposal comes in two parts, as the agenda indicates. Nicholas, Heir in von Schuss, and I, Karne, Lharr in Halarek, request that the Council of Starker IV enforce its sentence on Richard, duke-designate in Harlan, in whatever way is necessary to keep him in solitary confinement. Lord Nicholas and I made our retreat at Breven this year. We saw with our own eyes that Richard Harlan lives in luxury in a suite of rooms on Breven's lowest level and entertains vassals and allies there. He is *not* in penitential confinement. He is *not* in solitary confinement. We *saw*. If there's to be no enforcement, there is no sentence and Richard may as well live at home."

"No!" shouted some voices from the minor Houses.

"Where's von Schuss, then?" jeered a voice from the Kingsland back benches.

Karne went on as if he had not heard. "We also request that Council depose the abbot of Breven for dereliction of his duties, most especially letting Richard Harlan live in a luxurious suite and entertain whomever he pleases. He's also shown favoritism to the nobility by the large and luxurious suites he assigns them. This violates all rules of The Way against distinctions of rank or wealth."

A murmuring had begun when Karne proposed enforcing Council sentence. He had known it would not be a popular idea; House Harlan was too powerful and too intermarried. The murmuring increased to normal speaking levels when he mentioned Richard's luxury and rose to a roar when he cited the abbot's violations of the rules of The Way. Karne had to stop while the chairman gaveled the Council back into quiet. He wished he knew if the roar meant approval of his position or disapproval.

Karne aimed his next remark at the Freemen. He had learned from Duval that Freemen lived by a much stricter moral standard than the lords of Starker IV, especially the lords of the Nine, and knew the next revelation would hit them hard. "I have said Richard lives in luxury, and not alone. What I have not said is that his company often includes a whore. A woman in Breven, lords and Freemen." Karne did not wait for the roar of outrage—clearly from the Freemen's section this time—to die down but shouted over it. "This itself is bad enough—realize also that the abbot permitted it—but yesterday, lords and Freemen, yesterday Richard Harlan forced my sister Kathryn, who is wife to Lord Richard's own cousin Ennis, into Breven to be his whore."

The chamber exploded into sound and motion. If being a whore was bad by Freemen's standards, committing adultery—especially forcing adultery on an unwilling woman—was far worse.

Karne limped from behind his table. "Look you, lords and Freemen, at the wounds I bear." He turned slowly so all present could see his bloody hosen and the red and weeping skin of his burned hand. "House Halarek and House von Schuss raided Richard Harlan's secret quarters at Breven last night. I'm injured. Many from all three Houses are dead." Karne raised his voice above the angry murmuring. "I don't like the idea of soldiers in Breven any better than you, lords and Freemen, but what were we to do? Lord Richard was well-guarded by soldiers of Harlan. And he had my sister."

The murmuring changed its tone and grew louder. Karne roared over the noise, letting his frustration and rage provide volume. "My sister was there, lords and Freemen. My *sister!* For Richard's use. And she the honest wife of his own cousin!"

Men stamped and shouted then. They stood on their benches and poured into the aisles. They shook fists in the direction of the Harlan and Odonnel sections. Garren Odonnel's face lost its confident smile and wrinkles spread across his forehead. The Lord of the Mark, speaker for Harlan's vassal-trustees, had been standing to be recognized. He sat down again.

Gashen pounded his gavel again and again and again and again. "The proposals from Halarek are on the floor," he cried into the storm. "Does anyone want to speak to these issues before we vote?"

That was a formula question. The uproar faded to a loud murmur and got no quieter.

The Heir in Gormsby, a portly middle-aged man, stood with great dignity. "We have here a question of deep portent for the political and economic future of our world. The Duke of Harlan is a powerful man and dangerous to cross . . ." He droned on and on and on with many long words and very little content.

A young man on the Justin back benches shouted, "A virtuous wife, abducted for *pleasure*, and you talk about 'dangerous to cross'—"

The Earl of Justin turned and silenced the young man with a look. The young man stared back a moment, unrepentant, then sat down.

"There is an eight-minute limit on speeches, Lord Meer," Gashen told the Heir courteously. "You have one minute left. Please get to the point."

The Heir puffed up, offended. "I'll only say that Breven is the business of the governing Session of The Way and not of civilians."

"Point of order." A Freeman from Loch stood at a speaker's post in the aisle near his seat.

Gashen looked at him. "Your point, sir?"

"The Council has always had the power to remove abbots and even bishops who abuse their power, Chairman Gashen."

"Point well taken. Anyone else?"

Freemen began popping up like water on hot coals.

"He was sentenced to solitary confinement. Isn't he confined?"

"What does the abbot have to do with this?"

"Where was the fighting?"

"What were the casualties?"

Karne looked over his shoulder at the chairman, who nodded permission to speak. "The most important question first. The fighting was in Breven's lowest level and in the Old Ones' tunnel adjacent to it. Lord Richard had furnished a room in the tunnel for Lady Kathryn. He had also kept his whore from Loch there.

"Casualties—I don't know. I left as soon as the fighting stopped. We were fighting in very close quarters, though, so I'd guess most of the men there were at least wounded.

"About the abbot—the abbot has separated nobles and Freemen and provided the nobility with very large quarters, luxurious furnishings, and deacons for servants."

Karne then described the luxurious room Nik had been assigned. He had not finished before rows and rows of Freemen began to seethe. Many Freemen stood at their places and shouted for recognition or for the abbot's head. Lords from minor Houses were on their feet, at speakers' posts in the aisles, and in their places among the benches, shouting at the Nine, waving their arms, and calling for the chairman's attention. The commotion reassured Karne. It meant the other Retreat Houses were run as they should be. He himself had not had time for a retreat since his return from Balder, so he had not been sure. He returned to the Halarek prep table and sat down.

Chairman Gashen looked grim and satisfied at the same time, but few besides Karne were watching the chairman. Gashen was not partisan, not as the Marquis of Gormsby had been, but he had strong political opinions. The marquis's partisanship in Harlan's favor, even after Richard had committed murder in the Council chamber, was the reason the Freemen and minor Houses had voted together for the first time and taken forever the right of the Nine to the chairmanship.

Karne watched Old Party men, Freemen, and lords of minor Houses shouting at each other. This time the vote would go his way. Richard had gone too far. Ennis could go safely back to Holding McNeece, his testimony unnecessary, his presence here unrevealed.

In the end, not even an impassioned speech by Garren Odonnel defending the right to vengeance, whatever form that vengeance took, could turn the flood. By the time Council adjourned, it had voted to fine the abbot heavily and remove him from his post for three years. Council ordered Richard into a cell such as all retreat-makers were supposed to use and set up clock-round guarding by Council soldiers. Council also voted to station two troops at Breven to provide those guards, these to be sent as soon as they could be assembled. A squad of soldiers from those normally on duty on Council ground left immediately to take over the military cleanup. The coalition had won.

Karne stood slowly, using the tabletop to lever himself up. He wished he could rejoice in the victory, but his body ached and burned from wounds and the effort of battle, hunger gnawed at his stomach, his head ached with the tension of the meeting just finished, his heavy eyelids told him he had had no sleep in two days, and he felt sick with worry about Nik and Kit. All he wanted to do was eat and sleep and get back to Breven. But there were yet thanks to be said and farewells made.

He straightened with effort and turned to leave. A small page in von Schuss livery was shoving his way toward the central open area through the departing Council members, ignoring the curses and blows that followed him. He tugged at Karne's sleeve as if he thought that was necessary to catch Karne's attention.

"Lord Karne, my master bids you come. He has urgent words for your ears alone." He gave Karne's sleeve another jerk.

Karne pulled free impatiently. "Now?"

"At once, if you please, my lord."

If the baron had urgent news, he had heard something from Breven. Karne followed the page out of the chamber and to one of the small conference rooms on the outer diameter of the circular hall. Baron von Schuss sat in one of the straight-backed chairs, his head in his hands. He did not look up when Karne came in.

"There's been a rockfall. An Old Ones' trap."

Everything in Karne jerked tight. His jaw was so stiff he did not know if he could speak. The controller had not worked. "Kit?" he managed to get out. "Nik?"

"No one knows." The baron handed Karne a note as a blind man might, searching in the direction of Karne's voice.

The note said that everyone in the Retreat House had heard and felt something very heavy fall in the tunnel. After the dust settled, soldiers had gone very carefully into the tunnel to see what had happened. They found a sprung pit trap with two

Harlan soldiers in it, just as the survivors reported. Several hundred meters beyond, a slab of rock closed off further passage. Part of a Harlan soldier stuck out from under it. One of the searchers climbed the slab to see if there was any way through. He was sure he heard a piercing whistle from the other side, but there had been no sound since.

Karne gripped the back of the chair while the world went black. He lowered his head to restore blood-flow to it so he wouldn't fall. He should have known better than to take an untested device. Now he *had* to get through that mass of people in the corridor and back to Breven. He had to get back without revealing either his own state of mind or House Halarek's now desperate situation.

At least out there I can lean against a wall, he thought, and use the feel of it as a focus point. It'll help keep my mind here instead of at Breven.

Karne opened the conference room door and went out into the crowd. Well-wishers patted his shoulders or arms, shook his hand, complimented him on a fight well-organized and well-run. It was sort of like his first Council meeting, just after his return home, when he had also won against high odds and had used a wall's support to keep himself functioning. He maintained the pose of normality, as he had then, smiling wearily, laughing a little at friends' jokes, making small talk until the crowds were gone. Finally only he and Koort, Konnor, McNeece, and von Schuss were left, plus their secretaries, administrators, and other necessary officials.

Arlen of Koort shook Karne's hand, but did not let go immediately, almost as if he forgot he still held on. "This is a long fight, Karne Halarek. This was only one battle in it."

"My lord, I know."

"I realize it took me a long time to make up my mind, but you can count on me now, Karne Halarek. I, too, believe Richard is dangerous to more than House Halarek. And this debate is but the first of many."

Karne allowed himself a faint smile. This tall and lugubrious lord *had* taken a long time to ally himself, but he would be steady. "Then we must hold onto our allies, my lord, and win more."

"Just so." Arlen of Koort gave Karne's hand one last shake and moved on down the hall.

McNeece took the lift to the lower levels. The rest of the group moved off toward the pad and their fliers.

"Contact Breven," Karne muttered. "Important." His eyes slid shut and he did not know how much time he had lost before he realized he was asleep, though walking.

"You're out on your feet, Karne," the baron scolded. "Even you can see that. Let Tane fly your craft home. I'll take you home with me and I'll contact the retreat the moment we're in the air. Show some sense, son. Sleep."

Childreth Konnor glanced at his chrono. "It's very late and none of us have eaten since fast-breaking. I offer all of you the hospitality of my House this night." His smile included McNeece, who was just rejoining the group, and the stocky, hooded figure with him, in the invitation. "Durlene employs an excellent cook and my beds are soft and warm. . . ."

Karne considered the offer, his brain running as slowly as honey in Uhl. Konnor Holding was on the way to Breven and he *was* tired, so very, very tired, too tired to fly safely. The offer of food, too, especially Durlene of Konnor's food—. But his heart said to go at once to Breven.

The hooded figure cleared its throat and spoke in a husky whisper that was recognizable as Ennis's only if one knew he was in the vicinity. "I must decline. My wife is having some trouble. . . ."

The group shuffled uncomfortably. Childreth's hospitality was world-famous. Ennis turned to Karne.

"If you would accept my service as pilot, my lord, you could get to Breven quickly and safely."

Karne did not want to ride with this clan enemy. Yet they were brothers-in-law, no matter how unwillingly Kit had married, and Ennis's life was in far more danger in Breven and on the way there than Karne's was. Ennis would be no danger to him, and his offer would get Karne to Breven in just hours.

"Thanks," he said, deliberately omitting Ennis's name. He looked apologetically at Baron von Schuss. "Peace be on all your Houses." He bowed to the company, then followed Ennis to the pad, where they found a McNeece flitter waiting.

Prearranged protective coloration, Karne told himself.

He fastened himself into the safety webbing, leaned back, and let his eyes fall shut. At first his mind went round and round, worrying at the Old Ones' trap and defying the weariness of his body. *Traps like that suffocate. Nik and Kit alive? Maybe? Only heard one whistle from the other side. And Ennis? Cuckolded? Not? Loves Kit very much. Nik loves Kit very much. And I do. Wrong about Nik and love. Love muddled his thoughts. Muddles mine, too, though. Ennis loves Kit very much. Was wrong. Not just lovey-love ties a man in knots. Brother love, too. Weakens. Enemies can use against House. Love for Kit a hole in Halarek defenses. Weak spot. Ennis. Nik. Weak spot.*

Karne knew there was something important in the whirling thoughts that he should work out, but his mind kept slipping into sleep, and finally he could no longer pull himself back out.

By the time the flier touched down at Breven, Karne had had several hours sleep. His battered body, however, had stiffened considerably and even walking felt painful. He needed a ladder to get down from the flitter's wing, like an old man.

When Ennis saw how slowly Karne was moving, he said, "I can't wait. I'm sure you understand." He looked at Karne sharply. "No, you don't, do you? You will. Someday, you will." And Ennis sprinted off across the courtyard.

The words sounded so prophetic, they gave Karne a superstitious shiver. He hurried after Ennis as fast as he was able, praying all the while that there would be no need of fighting this trip, because he had no speed or flexibility left.

The scene on the lower level was not encouraging. Harsh Torchlight made stark contrasts. Men clambered over the slab of rock, picking up and carrying off whatever pieces of broken rock they could. Very small pieces of rock clittered over the slab and onto the stone floor whenever the men moved. The light washed out the color of their uniforms and cast their shadows in deep black on the walls behind them. Karne's chief Specials engineer told him they were waiting for miners from Melevan and their specialized tools. The rock slab was so hard they had not even been able to get an air line through with the equipment available. The man's voice could barely be heard over the whirr and whump of the generator that supplied power to the lights and tools, but the gist seemed to be that Orkonan had already sent for Melevan's miners, who would come because their overlord commanded it. The entire work area smelled of rock dust and dampness and sweat.

Karne watched in the wavering shadows. There was so much to do and so little time. Air. How much air was behind that rock and how long would it last? Such traps were designed to suffocate. House Halarek was dying, not at Harlan hands, but at the hands of long-dead Old Ones. Despair washed over him like a black wave.

CHAPTER 17

The dust settled thick on the floor and left a haze in the air. I ran our Torch's beam across the surface of the stone on the Breven side and then the stone on the tunnel side. They were both smooth and slightly glossy. Neither had cracks. Neither had lost even small bits of rock in their fall and they both fit so tightly that no light came through from the other side. There would be no fresh air coming in. The air in our small enclosed space was all the air we had. How long would it last? Minutes? Hours? Days? I didn't want it to last days. Facing certain death, I didn't want it to come that slowly.

"Do you want to leave the light on?" Nik's voice was hoarse and shook a little.

Did I? Did we want to watch each other die? That was what he was really asking. Or did I want to die in the dark? I didn't know which I wanted. No air was going to come through those rocks. We were going to suffocate, just as so many others had. Gasping for air, eyes bulging, fingers clawing at the rock until they wore down to the bone—that's how others died in these traps. Only they knew if they screamed. I wanted to scream and scream and scream, just to relieve the panic that was making my body shake and my stomach roll. The air already seemed thicker, harder to breathe. I shut my eyes and tried to calm myself.

The air doesn't go this fast, I told myself. You're scaring yourself. Breathe slowly and easily.

"The air will last for several hours, at least," Nik said, as if he were reading my thoughts.

I opened my eyes, still struggling to conquer my panic. Nik touched my cheek with cold, trembling fingers, then took the light and pushed himself up off the floor. He walked to the rock on the Breven side. Using the light and his free hand, he went over all the rock's edges carefully, as high as he could reach along the sides first, and then along the bottom. I knew this was something he had to do. I also knew there was no use in it. The Old Ones meant their traps to kill.

I stared at that rock and thought of all the dreams I had had for my life. Husband and children. A smallholding of my own to run. Love and respect from friends, family, and allies as I grew into old age. Well, I wasn't going to get old.

I thought about Narra. She would be forever caught between Harlan and Halarek, with no mother to give her advice or comfort. Ennis and Karne would keep her safe, though. Despite the ancient Family feud, I knew they would find a way to keep Narra safe. But I would never see her again, never hold her, or hear her cry or laugh or see her grow up . . .

I shut my eyes again, as if that would help stop the pain. I heard Nik's boots shushing faintly through the dust and the click of the Torch against rock and then Nik's soft cursing. I looked at him. He stood with his forehead against the rock on the tunnel side. The Torch hung from his limp right arm, his left hand pressed against the rock as if he could push it out of the way. His uneven breathing put odd pauses in the stream of curses. He turned until he was resting his back against the wall. The flow of curses stopped and Nik slowly sagged to the floor.

"There's no break. Not a one," he whispered. His voice cracked. "We're dead."

Dead. Dead. Dead. The word beat through my brain like a drum. This was not a nightmare. This was real. There was no hope. Only slow suffocation by the light of a Torch.

The air seemed thicker again. Maybe Nik's efforts had used extra oxygen. Maybe the thickness was my imagination. Maybe.

Nik looked at me with haunted eyes. "I brought you down a tunnel of the Old Ones to save your life and I've killed you instead."

I couldn't bear the pain in his voice. "Nik, you kept me from Richard—"

I had a brief flash of what Richard had done to me in front of his men. He would have done much more—humiliating things, painful things—on Council morning. I couldn't think of that and be brave as a woman of the Nine was supposed to be. Richard would have hurt me, a lot, and with pleasure. I knew deep inside that, after Richard, I would never have been able to enjoy coupling again.

Those thoughts were steps into nightmare and I could neither face them nor make them go away. I needed help to make them go away. I needed comfort in the face of dying. I scuttled across the floor to Nik, laid my head on his shoulder, and put my arms around him.

"Hold me, Nik," I whispered, near tears. "I'm so afraid."

Nik put his arms around me slowly, as if he were afraid to. They tightened cautiously. I looked up at his face to see what he was thinking. His face was tight with pain. His hand began rubbing the back of my neck gently. I snuggled my face into his neck and absorbed comfort from his solidity. His hand continued massaging my neck, his arm around me tightened. I felt the trembling and warmth of desire starting in me. Under my cheek, his heart beat more rapidly. His touch on my neck changed, became more caress than massage. He wanted me, too! Nik bent his head toward mine, then his arms loosened, and he straightened as if he were going to pull away from me.

I couldn't have borne that. I needed his warmth, his solidity, his love. "Nik, please," I whispered against his neck, "I need to be close to you. Don't make me die alone."

The feel of his neck under my lips stirred me. I had desired him so long. So long. I burrowed closer. His hands stroked my back gently. I wanted to move against him, to arouse him as he was arousing me. One hand slid to my side, then up. It paused in a caress that made me press against his hand and whimper a little in spite of myself. Pray the Guardians he wouldn't stop!

His hand slid up to my shoulder and around my neck. He tipped my head back and kissed me, a long, soft kiss that I thought would stop my heart. He looked down at me, his dark eyes dilated with desire.

"This is wrong, Kit," he said slowly. "The Four Guardians know how long I've wanted you, but you're Ennis's wife."

"We can't hurt him, Nik: We're as good as dead. We're going to suffocate, just like everyone else who's run into one of these traps. All Ennis will be able to do with me the next time he sees me is bury me. Is it really wrong to give each other comfort in the time we have left?"

I nibbled his neck with my lips. Honor and nobility are for the living. We were the dead. Once, just once in my life, I wanted pleasure with a man I loved. Surely the Guardians wouldn't sentence us to endless agony for that.

Nik drew a deep, shaky breath. "Kit, you're tempting me beyond my resistance."

"Good," I said against the soft skin where neck joins shoulder. "I need comforting, Nik. I need forgetting. If my breaths get shallower and quicker, I want to believe it's from desire and not slow suffocation. *Please*, Nik. I've loved you since I was fifteen. You know that."

His hands tightened. He kissed down my cheek and neck to my soft shoulder-place, while his hands did devastating things. "Guardians, forgive me." His voice was rough and stirred me almost as much as his touch. He paused a moment. "Do you want the light left on?" His hands kept moving, touching me, telling me his love and desire better than words.

Much as I wanted to watch his face and see his body as we coupled, I couldn't say yes. Not in this place. Not with death just around the corner. "I don't want to see the trap, Nik. I want to pretend for a little while."

Nik made a little sound, part sigh, part moan, turned off the Torch and pulled me as close to him as it was possible to get. We pretended there was no tunnel, no trap. We thought only of the feel and taste and scent of each other and the rocketing pleasure we created in that dark and terrible place. We coupled again and again in the dark, as often as the air and our energy allowed, making up for the years we would never have. The last thing I knew as unconsciousness closed in was the feel of Nik's warm, damp skin against my cheek.

I heard a voice, far away at first, then closer and closer. "Kit? Kit!"

It was Karne. Had Karne died, too?

Someone was shaking my shoulder. "Kit, talk to me!"

I took a deep breath and coughed. There was air, and Karne's urgent voice. Maybe I wasn't dead. He wouldn't sound worried if both of us were dead. I opened my eyes slowly. Karne was kneeling beside me, his forehead wrinkled, his eyes concerned.

"The Allfather be praised!" Karne said. His hand stroked my cheek.

I propped myself up on one elbow. No sleeves hindered my rising. No dress pulled against the movement. Then I remembered. Nik and I had been loving each other up to our last conscious moment. We had nothing on.

I glanced quickly around for clothes. Beyond Karne, Dr. Othneil was bending over Nik, who was beginning to stir. I looked at Karne.

"Melevan's miners were the first ones through," he said, in answer to my unspoken question. "There wasn't a lot of doubt about what you two had been doing. We'll deal with that later. Can you get up?"

"If I have clothes on." I noticed Karne wasn't looking lower than my face.

Karne reached over me and scraped together my clothes. They were dusty beyond belief. I was dusty beyond belief. I shook out my underslip and put it on. Now, at least, I was decent. The effort took a lot of energy. I sat down at once and rested my head against my raised knees. Karne put a hand on my shoulder. It was very comforting.

"I have some bad news," Karne said. "Ennis is dead. He came here to help and an assassin burned him. The assassin had been in von Schuss as a soldier at least ten years, waiting until his master called for his special skills. The baron hasn't learned yet how Richard turned the man to Harlan, but he will."

Karne's voice held a grim determination that I knew would seem pale beside Emil's. Yes, the assassin would tell Emil what he wanted to know. I felt an unwelcome relief at the news about Ennis. With Ennis dead, what Nik and I had done could not be called adultery, and what we had done would soon be public knowledge. No one finds two naked people wrapped around each other and assumes there's some innocent explanation. After that unworthy thought, I felt grief. Ennis had not deserved to die. Tears crept down my cheeks and left a salty, dusty taste at the corners of my mouth.

Karne's voice softened. "I'm sorry, Kit. Ennis was a brave and honest man."

I let myself mourn for him then in the way of my people, high keenings that would tell everyone within earshot that I grieved for my husband. Only a thin wail echoed back. I didn't have the strength to give cry for him properly. Ennis, of the dry humor and skillful hands, was dead. Ennis, my friend and rescuer. He had come to Breven to help, knowing how dangerous it would be for him. And Richard had had him killed.

Karne put his arm around me and let me mourn. Soon my voice could wail no more. Then came fear. I was a widow again, a *thing* to be fought over: A highborn widow is always a target for strong and ambitious men and is unlikely to be able to hold out against them without the help of a powerful House. Halarek was not a powerful House just now. Our four-year war against Harlan had consumed vast portions of our capital, though Halarek had won. What House was strong enough to risk taking me in, a woman twice widowed, with the shadow of war with Harlan hanging over her?

Karne was shaking my shoulder. "Come on, Kit! You can mourn him more safely at home. It's time to get out of here." He stood and extended a hand to help me up.

Suddenly I didn't want to leave this place. It would have been better to die here than to go out into the savagery of Gharr politics, especially since I would again be a pawn in the game and not a piece with power. I rested my forehead on my upraised knees again and shook my head. Karne crouched beside me.

"Don't be absurd, Kit. This place is still dangerous. You have to leave."

I looked up at him. He understood what I was thinking. We've always been close that way.

"Don't be afraid, Kit. Richard's locked up under clock-round guard, in a real retreat room. The order to kill Ennis had to have gone out weeks ago.'' He pulled me up, wrapped his arms around me, and spoke into my ear. ''I promised you to Nik if he found you. No one expected Ennis to live long after he helped you escape, and he didn't. Ennis knew the price he'd pay. You'll take the necessary forty days for mourning, then you'll marry Nik. Once the story of how you and he were found gets out, you'll have no other option.'' He pulled back to look me in the face. ''You aren't sorry that's your only option, I hope.''

I couldn't speak. This kind of blessing doesn't often happen to a woman of the Houses. I hugged Karne hard. He hugged back, then started us toward the narrow channel of light from Breven. I felt as thin as grass, and I sagged against him as if I had no strength left. What strength I did have was flowing into joy.

Karne hugged me tighter. ''I have you back. I was afraid I was the last Halarek.''

He pushed me into the narrow passageway ahead of him, but he kept a strong grip along my waist as we inched through to the outside. The lights and noise on the Breven side stopped me for a moment until my eyes and senses could adjust. Nik already stood outside, supported by two Halarek Blues. He smiled at me like sunshine. Seeing that smile, and other faces, and hearing other voices—it was almost more than I could bear without crying, and crying in front of anyone not personal family is a disgrace. I was alive. My brother was alive. Our House would survive.

I wrapped one arm around Karne for balance and raised the other into the air, fist clenched. The fist wavered rather unvaliantly. ''Halarek lives!'' I shouted, my voice cracking in my parched throat.

Melevan's miners, and the Blues farther down the tunnel toward Breven, shot their fists into the air, too, and shouted that battle cry until the tunnel boomed with it. ''Halarek lives! Halarek lives!''

CLASSIC SCIENCE FICTION
AND FANTASY

__DUNE Frank Herbert 0-441-17266-0/$4.95
The bestselling novel of an awesome world where gods and
adventurers clash, mile-long sandworms rule the desert, and
the ancient dream of immortality comes true.

__STRANGER IN A STRANGE LAND Robert A. Heinlein
0-441-79034-8/$5.95
From the *New York Times* bestselling author—the science
fiction masterpiece of a man from Mars who teaches
humankind the art of grokking, watersharing and love.

__THE ONCE AND FUTURE KING T.H. White
0-441-62740-4/$5.95
The world's greatest fantasy classic! A magical epic of King
Arthur in Camelot, romance, wizardry and war. By the author
of *The Book of Merlyn*.

__THE LEFT HAND OF DARKNESS Ursula K. LeGuin
0-441-47812-3/$4.50
Winner of the Hugo and Nebula awards for best science fiction
novel of the year. "SF masterpiece!"—*Newsweek* "A Jewel of
a story."—Frank Herbert

__MAN IN A HIGH CASTLE Philip K. Dick 0-441-51809-5/$3.95
"Philip K. Dick's best novel, a masterfully detailed alternate
world peopled by superbly realized characters."
—Harry Harrison